THE LEGACY SERIES

Maximum Speed
Kevin Clouther

Reach Her in This Light
Jane Curtis

The Spirit in My Shoes
John Michael Cummings

*The Effects of Urban Renewal on Mid-Century America and
Other Crime Stories*
Jeff Esterholm

What Makes You Think You're Supposed to Feel Better
Jody Hobbs Hesler

Fugitive Daydreams
Leah McCormack

Hoist House: A Novella & Stories
Jenny Robertson

Finding the Bones: Stories & A Novella
Nikki Kallio

Self-Defense
Corey Mertes

Where Are Your People From?
James B. De Monte

Sometimes Creek
Steve Fox

The Plagues
Joe Baumann

The Hopefuls is a beautiful collection about what happens after the dreams of true love, elite instructors, and academic jobs crash against the ballast of dwindling economies and cheating partners. "Every year the hopeful wave comes in, shining and eager, but by the following year, especially among the poets, the tide turns." Oness is too good a storyteller to leave it there. With her literary eye and attention to our current unease, Oness writes about the surprising ways the vulnerable and misunderstood are taken down or survive that pulling tide. In "Look Both Ways," Kevin's need to get home is interrupted by other people's requests and predicaments. In helping strangers, he touches on a quiet dignity at his core, one that seemed lost in the noise and friction of expectations. This masterful work resonates with the creative ways we might, like Kevin, see our lives anew.

—MAUREEN AITKEN
author of *The Patron Saint of Lost Girls*

THE HOPEFULS

stories ELIZABETH ONESS

CORNERSTONE PRESS
UNIVERSITY OF WISCONSIN-STEVENS POINT

Cornerstone Press, Stevens Point, Wisconsin 54481
Copyright © 2025 Elizabeth Oness
www.uwsp.edu/cornerstone

Printed in the United States of America by
Point Print and Design Studio, Stevens Point, Wisconsin

Library of Congress Control Number: 2025934055
ISBN: 978-1-960329-84-4

Cornerstone Press titles are produced in courses and internships offered by the Department of English at the University of Wisconsin–Stevens Point.

DIRECTOR & PUBLISHER
Dr. Ross K. Tangedal

EXECUTIVE EDITORS
Jeff Snowbarger, Freesia McKee

EDITORIAL DIRECTOR
Brett Hill

SENIOR EDITOR
Ellie Atkinson

PRESS STAFF
Cora Bender, Paige Biever, Andrew Glazer, Lillian Kulbeck, Sam Zajkowski, Anthony Thiel, Kimberly Janesch, Sophie McPherson, Madison Schultz, Autumn Vine, Ava Willett

ALSO BY ELIZABETH ONESS:

FICTION
Leaving Milan
Twelve Rivers of the Body
Departures
Articles of Faith

POETRY
Fallibility
Sure Knowledge

CONTENTS

I

Protect and Serve

In March, they started appearing everywhere: the Dalai Lama, Gandhi, Martin Luther King, Che Guevara, their photocopied faces tacked to phone poles in the neighborhood. Probably some college kid doing it, Ramsey thought, a protest against the war, which seemed inevitable now. He'd noticed the signs in his own neighborhood first—Gandhi's skinny face taking up a whole page, Martin Luther King didn't copy well, Che Guevara (secretly, Ramsey was pleased he knew who Che was) all tacked to poles near the university. He wondered if the protester was baiting him, some kid he'd arrested trying to have the last word.

Then, like a bad case of chicken pox, the pictures spread—in front of the coffee house, at all the major intersections—faces pocking the residential neighborhoods. He hadn't thought of chicken pox in years, funny they should occur to him now, but both his kids had gotten them bad—Bruce first, a few dots on his face, then they'd covered his torso. Kathy had been the same way: a few dots appeared on her stomach, then blisters bloomed all over her body. He'd told his wife that he hoped they would avoid Kathy's face, spare her those small, pitted scars, and Lucy, with a maternal wisdom she seemed to have lost, had said, "Let's not let her look in the mirror. Maybe she won't scratch as much if she can't see how bad it is," and the blisters had finally faded with calamine and Benadryl.

Bruce was in the Marines now, still in training, but of course he'd be called up. Kathy was at the Senior High, pissed about Bruce enlisting, but she was pissed about everything now. Yesterday she came home with blue hair. Part of being a cop's kid, he supposed. Occasionally he had to tell her to watch her attitude, but part of him was glad for her rebellious anger. He wanted a daughter who was tough.

People thought that being a cop in a small town was easy, but they didn't know. Town wasn't that small any-more—20,000 with the outlying rural areas—and the college kids added another seven or eight thousand. The students came with their own set of problems—drunk driv-ing, property damage, pissing on people's lawns—but those were predictable. Everything was more complicated than it had been twenty years ago. Now, you had to be careful about blood. Even at a traffic accident, you had to put on gloves. Any threats at the high school had to be taken seriously. Ramsey sighed, scratched the tuft of hair above his left ear. There had been guns everywhere when he was a kid, but if he'd touched his father's gun, the old man would have broken his arm. Kids didn't have the same sense of prohibi-tion now. Since Columbine, and that mess up in Pine Ridge, you could never be too careful. The man he'd assigned to the high school was good, knew how to keep his ears open, and Ramsey tried not to give in to the vague feeling that the inmates had overtaken the asylum. There was the whole meth thing too—they'd busted five labs over the winter—so this thing with the pictures didn't seem like a big deal, at first.

HE POURED HIMSELF a cup of coffee, glanced at the ther-mometer outside the back window, 37 degrees, and sat down at the kitchen table. Minnesota had been colder when he was a kid. Now, March was muddy, still raw, but the expectation of warmth hovered in the air. Across the table, wisps of blue hair waved above the local paper. He recognized her ruse: if she acted like a grown-up, reading the paper, he couldn't accuse her of being sullen.

"So, Kath, what do you think about these pictures?"

She turned the page.

"I asked you a question, young lady."

She lowered the paper, pointed to her full and moving cheek. After a minute, she swallowed. "What pictures?"

"You know, the Dalai Lama, Gandhi, those ones."

"Haven't seen them." She folded the paper, cleared her plate, and headed off to school.

Ramsey sighed and pulled the paper toward him. He couldn't press his point without calling her a liar.

THE FACES LOOKED OVER him as he drove into work. Near the county building, someone had drawn a curly mustache on the Dalai Lama. Pushing on the double doors, the sound of querulous debate floated up the hall. His men, well, he couldn't say 'men' anymore, they had a woman on the force, stopped talking when he opened the door.

"Morning, everyone," Ramsey said.

"Morning." Gundersen spoke for the group. "We figure you've seen them—what do you want us to do about those signs?"

"Take 'em down if you happen to be walking the neighborhood, but otherwise, ignore them."

"It's disrespectful in these times," Owens said.

"Well," Ramsey said. "It's just someone having their say."

"Isn't there a town ordinance against posting bulletins on phone poles?" Owens stuck his head forward, as if sniffing for something he couldn't see.

"Technically, people aren't supposed to put up anything— auction notices, diet ads, garage sale signs, but we've got other things to think about." Ramsey sat down at his desk, indicating the discussion was over.

"So, take them down if we're in the neighborhood?" Owens asked.

Ramsey looked up at him. "Have I been speaking English, Owens?"

At the end of the day, driving home, Ramsey noticed that the poles had been stripped of their faces. He wondered if his men's thoroughness came from their own convictions, or if they thought this would please him.

KATHY WAS AT SWIM PRACTICE. Lucy had left dinner out for him. The empty house made Ramsey think of night. All winter, he'd had trouble sleeping. He told himself it was because Lucy was out in the evenings, more and more, now. She was involved with some community theater group, and their rehearsals ran late. Over the years, her bursts of enthusiasm had lasted for indeterminate stretches, then shifted, as if she'd never taken part in what had absorbed her so fully. When the kids were younger, raising them had consumed her, then it was quilting, then a brief flirtation with gardening; now she was making costumes, gathering props.

He decided to walk after dinner, hoping it would help him sleep later on. He put on an old pair of khaki pants, a white sweatshirt, sneakers, and let himself out of the house. Nelson Mandela smiled down at him from a phone pole by the corner of his lawn. Had it been there when he came home? He wasn't sure.

Block by block, he knew the tenor of the neighborhoods. His grandmother had lived in a little house down on Eighth Street. The house had been sold long ago, rented to losers who kept ratty furniture on the porch. There'd been a domestic assault there last month. Ramsey strode briskly, the damp cold of the sidewalk seeping up through his sneakers. Television sets glowed in living rooms; the squares of light, facing different directions, lit the rooms with shifting images: women in low-cut tops running through a city, someone jumping off a cliff, people in bathing suits running through a jungle. Everyone had cable now. A million channels and nothing to watch. Or all the same thing, depending on how you looked at it. Reality TV. Why did they put stupid people on television? So other stupid people would watch?

Someone moved at the end of the block, and Ramsey stepped onto the grass so he could approach without being heard. A bulky figure, standing on tip-toe, was balanced on a stool, fixing a picture to a phone pole. It looked like a woman and, as he got closer, he saw she wasn't heavy, merely bundled in a lumpy coat. A backpack, which he supposed contained the signs, rested on the ground. She reached above her head then turned to look over her shoulder as he approached. A flash of white across her face. She held a card of tacks in her teeth.

"Hi there," he said.

She pushed on a tack above Gandhi and turned, taking the card out of her mouth.

"Hi." Her voice was low and pleasant. She got down from her stool.

He was suddenly aware of his hands, stiff and cold, and he put them in his sweatshirt pockets. Out of uniform, he felt disguised. "I've seen your signs around," Ramsey said.

She smiled at the corner of her mouth. She looked like a Madonna, not the singing one, a real one, with long, dark hair, her hood fallen back. It was hard to tell in the dark, but she seemed older than a college student.

"Why do you use a stepstool?"

"I want them to be high enough so they can't be ripped down."

He smiled at her miscalculation. She wasn't much more than five feet tall. The signs were easily within a tall man's reach. He could tear one down himself.

She picked up the stepstool and started down the block. He looked for a car idling, didn't see one, and followed her down the sidewalk.

"Do you think they'll make a difference?"

"I hope so."

She walked quickly, and he fell in step with her. "You've put up a lot of signs. Are you doing this by yourself?"

She glanced at him, then set her stepstool down at the next phone pole. He took her silence as reproof for his nosiness, or the seeming obviousness of the answer.

"You ask a lot of questions," she said.

"I'm curious."

"It's a curious world," she said.

Ramsey brushed something invisible off his sleeve. He sensed that revealing his position would put him at a disadvantage. The wind picked up, riffling the pictures inside her pack, cutting through his sweatshirt; he should have worn a windbreaker. Since there was no sign of a car, she must live somewhere in the neighborhood. He'd see her again.

"Well, good night," he said.

"Good night."

He headed down the block. Clouds blew across the quarter moon. He'd been out for longer than he thought. When he realized he'd forgotten to ask her name, he felt a sting of embarrassment.

As he stepped onto his front path, he saw Lucy's car was still out. Kathy sat in the living room, watching CNN.

"It sucks! It just sucks. Bush is steamrolling his way through. He should treat the United Nations with some respect."

Ramsey got himself a beer and sat down at the other end of the couch. "We pay for the United Nations."

"Then we should pay attention to it," Kathy said.

He was still surprised, pleased, when his children had opinions that were wholly their own. "Sometimes the only way to deal with a bully is to make a show of strength," Ramsey said.

Kathy looked at him directly. Her eyes, which used to be wide, astonished, were narrowed and analytical. Her pudgy nose seemed incongruous in her longish face. She was a smart kid, but her intelligence hadn't been shaped by experience yet. The blue in her hair was a shade lighter than yesterday; maybe the routine of swim practice would wash the dye out. As she studied him, challenging, it was hard to remember her as a soft, plushy child.

"You know, I'm not stupid. I do think Saddam Hussein is a bad guy, but we're going to go over there and bomb the shit out of them, and everyone will hate us for it."

He took a sip of beer. "Where's your mom?"

"At rehearsal for something crapulous."

A smile tugged at the corner of his mouth. "You shouldn't talk about her interests that way."

"You think those silly musicals are awful. You can admit it, at least to me."

She was curled on the couch, holding a pillow, her hair still damp from showering after practice. He opened his mouth to say something conciliatory, to revive their old camaraderie, but she stood up, threw the pillow to the side, and tossed him the remote.

"I can't take any more of this." She stomped upstairs to her room.

WHEN HE DROVE TO WORK the next morning, Ramsey saw how many pictures the woman had put up the previous night. She had chosen heavily trafficked areas: streets where students lived, the road near the café. Owens was at Ramsey's elbow the minute he walked in the door.

"They're at it again," Owens said.

"What's that?"

"Those pictures, all those peaceniks."

"Peaceniks? Like sputniks?"

Owens looked puzzled for a moment, then shifted the gum he was chewing to the other side of his mouth. A stupid habit, Ramsey thought, a grown man chewing gum.

"It's not funny. We've got to do something."

"Have you seen anyone putting them up?"

"No, they must be doing it at night."

"Helluva way to spend your evening," Ramsey said.

"I bet it's those people who protest down by the bank."

"The Peace Makers?"

"Yeah." Owens bunched his eyebrows together, as if he could see them in the distance.

"Owens, they're a bunch of professors, and people who dole out soup down at the *Catholic Worker*. They gather peaceably; they don't bother anyone." Ramsey glanced at last night's report. "Gerke brought two high school kids into the Emergency Room last night. Both of them high as hell. Had to cuff 'em just to get them to the hospital. They didn't have a car, so they're getting this stuff some place in town. I'd say that that's our bigger concern."

WITH BRUCE GONE, dinners at home were quiet. Lucy tried to make conversation, asking Kathy about her classes and teachers and friends. Kathy would tell her that Mary Lou had gotten pregnant and just had an abortion, or that someone's parents were getting divorced. Ramsey kept his head down. *Sleeping dogs*, he wanted to tell his wife, but he knew she'd take it the wrong way.

"I saw those pictures you were talking about," Kathy announced. She twirled spaghetti on her fork.

"My men have been taking them down, but they keep going up again."

"What right do they have to take them down?"

"Well, technically, there's an ordinance."

Kathy made an expression of disgust, and started to twirl another huge amount of spaghetti. "I think they're cool," she said, and gazed at Ramsey over her laden fork. Something in him quivered, as if she sensed what he was thinking.

Lucy put her face into her hands and burst into tears.

"Lucy, what is it?"

"Stop arguing. Just stop it."

"Lucy, we're not arguing."

"Of course you are." She got up and ran from the table.

Ramsey and Kathy looked at each other.

"You should talk to her," Kathy said.

Ramsey felt a weight in his legs. "Were we arguing?" he asked.

"She hears what we don't even say," Kathy said. "We know where we stand."

Ramsey put down his fork. "I'm tired of everyone being so damn sure of where I stand."

LUCY WAS IN HER SEWING ROOM, a place he'd fixed up for her when she announced her latest interest. She sat in front of her machine, pulling out a seam.

"I'd like a little time to myself," Lucy said. She turned to look at him, her face red with tears.

"Are you sure? I—"

"I'm tired of being the glue!" Lucy's mouth was open, as if to shout, but her words came out in a hoarse whisper.

"What?"

"If I didn't talk, you two would just sit there, shoveling food into yourselves without exchanging a civil word. I'm tired of trying to smooth things over! I'm tired of everyone thinking I'm ridiculous!" Her chin quivered. She looked away, pressed her trembling lips together.

"Lucy, we don't think you're ridiculous."

"Of course you do. *I* do! Do you think I can't hear myself?" The small light from the sewing machine shone on the raised veins and loose skin of her hand.

"She's worried about Bruce. Conversation isn't going to change that."

"I'd just like to finish what I'm working on." Looking down, Lucy smoothed a piece of shiny, peach-colored fabric in her lap.

"Are you sure?"

"Yes."

"I'm going out for a walk then," Ramsey said.

In the kitchen, Kathy was washing the dinner dishes, her face closed to him now. He changed his clothes and went out, locking the door behind him. The smell of wood smoke and melted snow drifted in the air. On Sioux Street, headlights flickered over the signs, which had been placed at random intervals along the road. At night, the drivers would barely see what they were passing.

He walked for almost two hours, pictures floating around him in the dark, before he finally admitted she might not be out. Mandela was still at the corner of his yard. Ramsey remembered seeing him released from jail—it had been on the news—and Ramsey had measured the years Mandela had been in jail against the span of his own life. So much time lost. Bruce was just a toddler then. Kathy hadn't been born.

When he let himself in, he expected Lucy to be sitting up, reading, but the lights were out, the bedroom window open. He brushed his teeth, undressed quickly and climbed into bed, reaching for her. She stirred, naked under the covers. When he touched her shoulder, she felt hot.

"Lucy," he whispered. "Are you awake? You feel like you have a fever."

She gave a dry laugh. "This is what it's like. You can't believe how hot I feel sometimes."

He got out of bed, the air cold on his stomach and thighs, and went into the bathroom for a washcloth. He ran it under cold water, wrung it out, and brought it back to the bedroom. He set it awkwardly against her neck.

"I knew you got these, but I didn't know they were so…"

"Really hot?"

"Yeah." He tried to pat her forehead with the washcloth. She pushed it off her eye. "Well, they are."

"Can I get you anything?"

"Roll back the clock twenty years," Lucy said.

THE FOLLOWING NIGHT, the air was warmer. Ramsey walked down Wabasha Street, past the house they'd lived in when Kathy was born. When Kathy was little, perhaps two years old, she'd sit next to him on the couch on Sunday afternoons while he watched football or basketball. The joke between them was that she just wanted potato chips, but she'd cuddle under his arm, sit with him in a way that Bruce had always been too restless to do. One day, Lucy came into the living room as Kathy was standing on the couch, peering at the top of Ramsey's head.

"Kiss Daddy on his bald spot," Lucy teased.

Kathy bent over and planted a kiss on the top of his head.

The cool moistness of her lips on his scalp was unexpected. Ramsey grinned, trying not to show that Lucy had hit a nerve. He could run, work out, try to stay in shape, but there was no help for the hair he washed down the drain every time he took a shower. Kathy kissing his bald spot became a family joke: she would climb onto the couch, stand on her toes, and plant a kiss on his head. *Daddy, daddy, daddy,* she would hug him and kiss his head, his cheek. Oh well, if he had to lose his hair, he could live with this. Bruce was more obstinate, wanting to make things true through simple insistence. Ramsey would tell him not to wipe his nose on his sleeve, not to hang on the banister, and Bruce would say, "I'm not," just as he was doing it.

As Bruce got older, Ramsey tried to instill in him the necessity of giving things your best shot. Bruce had played the usual sports: baseball, soccer, football, and basketball. He seemed to enjoy being part of a team. Although he liked to win, he was always a good sport, and Ramsey was proud of him—no pouting or sullenness. His son had a generosity of spirit that wasn't the kind of thing you could teach. He could accept that things didn't always go his way. In high school, Bruce decided not to play football, opting for soccer instead. Apparently, he'd fretted for weeks about whether Ramsey would be disappointed by this decision, and when Bruce finally told him, and Ramsey said that was fine, he'd been taken aback by the boy's relief. What had Ramsey done to inspire such trepidation? Mostly, he had the impression that Bruce didn't worry about what he thought. Ramsey had never told him, but he was actually relieved that Bruce didn't go out for football. High school sports didn't seem worth wracking up your body for.

Up ahead, a woman pushed a stroller down the sidewalk in the dark. As he moved closer, he saw a bundled baby asleep inside. The woman looked up, startled, then recognized him and set her stepstool near a phone pole. She pulled the Dalai Lama out of her backpack.

"Evening," Ramsey said.

"Hi."

"Does your baby sleep through this?"

"He wouldn't have to if your men didn't keep taking down my signs."

Ramsey stepped back. How had she learned who he was? He couldn't see her face in the dark.

"Well, there's an ordinance against posting signs on private property, and the phone poles belong to the phone company."

"Actually, since they don't contain lettering, they're not technically signs." She pushed a thumbtack above the Dalai Lama's head, the metallic gleam like a tiny halo.

"What are they then?"

"Images."

Sometimes, Ramsey wished he still smoked cigarettes. Pausing to light up had given him time to think without appearing to be at a loss.

"Signs are usually meant to communicate something," Ramsey said. "Don't your images do that?"

"People draw their own conclusions."

She slung her pack over her shoulder, picked up her stepstool, and pushed the stroller with one hand. She wore knitted gloves without fingers; they looked sexy on her small hands.

"Let me take that stepstool for you."

She tightened her arm, resisting.

"I didn't mean I was going to take it away. I meant 'let me carry it for you.'"

A streetlight shone down on her face, and she looked at him, surprised, and relaxed her arm. As he took the stool, he smelled her soap, or shampoo, drifting around him in the night air.

"Did you know I was a policeman before?"

"No."

They walked in silence, the sidewalks dark with ice and damp.

"Do you really think your pictures will change people's minds?" Ramsey asked.

"I hope they'll make people think."

Across the street, a family had posted a sign in their yard NO WAR IN IRAQ. Down the block, in a yard across the way, LIBERATE IRAQ.

"My son joined the Marines," Ramsey said.

"Did you want him to?"

"No." He had not admitted this to anyone, even to Lucy. "No." His voice seemed loud in the dark.

She put her hand on his upper arm. "It's time for me to go home now."

"I—" he didn't know what to say, but wanted to offer her something. "I don't tell my men to take down your signs. They do it on their own."

"You could tell them to stop," she said.

Standing in the clear air, he felt like a kid caught in a lie. She was right—his offering was flimsy. What prevented him from telling his men to leave the signs alone? Routine? Reputation? A few years ago, he was down in La Crosse with Bruce, and a man in fatigues and military boots who looked particularly fit came out of the food co-op. Ramsey guessed he worked at Fort McCoy. The man walked toward a car that Ramsey thought couldn't be his: a beat-up Volvo with a bumper sticker that said, COMFORT THE DISTURBED. DISTURB THE COMFORTABLE.

"Well, that's odd," he said to Bruce.

"What?" Bruce asked.

And Ramsey had suddenly been aware of how shallow his comment would have been.

THE PRESIDENT HAD GIVEN his ultimatum. In town, at work, at home, a constricted sense of expectation made Ramsey's legs feel heavy, as if he were trying to walk through water. Kathy wouldn't speak to him or Lucy, and when he finally prodded her about it, at dinner one night, she turned on him.

"It's your fault! It's all your fault! If he wasn't trying to please you, he wouldn't have joined!" Beneath her pale blue hair, Kathy's face looked angular, torn, as she shouted across the table.

Ramsey set down his glass. He got up from the table and left the house.

HE WALKED FOR HOURS, didn't return until late, when the house was dark. Kathy's door was closed. He hoped she was in her room, but didn't want to check. In their bedroom, Lucy snored softly. Ramsey undressed and lay still in the dark. He didn't expect to sleep.

When he woke the next morning and came down to breakfast, Kathy had already left for school. Lucy, her eyelids swollen, set a cup of coffee in front of him.

"Doesn't seem right to be rehearsing a Cole Porter play right now," she said.

He nodded, refrained from saying it had never seemed worth doing at all.

LATE THAT AFTERNOON, he was called to the Kwik Trip on Baker Street. Gundersen and Owens were already there. A fourteen-year-old kid had taken his parents' car and plowed into the front of the store. Luckily, no one was hurt, besides the kid himself, who'd busted up his leg, his collarbone, his face. The floor was covered with shattered glass, exploded bottles of soda, beef jerky and candy bars. The car's sideview mirror, stuck in a mangled display of Pringles, made his stomach feel oddly hollow. After the ambulance had taken the boy to the hospital, Ramsey drove down Baker Street toward the high school.

The sign woman stood at the intersection of Baker and Sarnia, talking to a girl with blue-blonde hair. From a distance, it took him a minute to register it was Kathy. She was so tall now, grown-up. He pulled up in the cruiser and got out.

In daylight he saw the woman had chapped lips, large, pale blue eyes. Her long hair was brown, no gray in it, but she looked older than she did at night. Kathy crossed her arms in front of her chest. Ramsey's stomach tightened, as if preparing to take a punch.

"Moved to daytime?" Ramsey said lightly.

"The times seemed to call for it." Her voice was youthful, her expression grave. Kathy looked back and forth between them, clearly caught off guard.

"My men, well, the force, tends to patrol this street, especially down toward Broadway. They should have had their fill of excitement today," and he nodded back toward the Kwik Trip, "but some of your signs would stay put a little longer if you worked the side streets, Howard and Mark, those kind of places," Ramsey said.

He touched his hat, feeling foolish at the old-fashioned gesture, then got back into the car.

WHEN HE GOT HOME after work, Lucy was out. He went into the living room where Kathy was sitting in the recliner, watching the beginning of the war on CNN.

"She said you'd met her before."

"I did."

"That you didn't make her take the signs down."

Ramsey nodded.

"It's sick," Kathy said. "That we can watch this."

It looked like fireworks on television. The muffled lights flashed like heat lightning, a decimated dawn. His legs felt like water. He sat down on the edge of the couch, feeling as if he couldn't draw a deep breath, as if something were squeezing his lungs. Kathy handed him the remote; she didn't protest when he flipped back and forth between Brokaw and Rather. They would send Bruce into that. Ramsey, who'd coached him his whole life about giving things your best shot, oh god, he'd done it, he knew how the Marines trained you, Bruce would go in and do what he'd been trained to do, for reasons that were noble and stupid, reasons that Ramsey knew well. Kathy sat in the recliner, pressed against the back, as if centrifugal force held her there, as if she were moving at terrific speed. Ramsey leaned his head onto his forearms and began to sob. He had set up his own son. He should have known. He should have wished for the rebelliousness in his son that he'd wished for in his daughter. His son would die, and it would be his fault. Something was breaking inside him; he pressed his face into his arms. His chest felt hot. He couldn't breathe.

Kathy moved toward him, put her hand on his back. "Dad? Daddy?"

Oh, how long since she'd spoken to him like this. *Daddy.* Something in him broke. He wheezed. His lungs ached. "It's my fault," he sobbed.

"I shouldn't have said it." Kathy was crying now. "I was angry. It's just everything. He might not even have to go over there. It might be over soon."

He hadn't cried like this since he was a child. He didn't want to pick up his head and look at his daughter.

She rubbed his shoulder. "I'm really sorry," she said. "I'm sorry, it's okay." She bent over him and kissed the top of his head, her lips dry, the wetness was tears. He started to cry again, remembering Lucy the other night, when he'd asked what he could do. *Turn back the clock twenty years.*

Kathy put her arm around his shoulders. He couldn't remember the last time she had touched him with affection. He picked up his head and touched the soft skin of his scalp, the patch without hair so much larger now.

"Remember when I used to do that? Kiss you on your bald spot?"

"Yes," Ramsey said. "I remember." He tried to smile, but he was still weeping. He grabbed a handful of tissues and sat back on the couch. She had said the worst she could say. Maybe it wouldn't be between them anymore. She leaned against him on the sofa. It seemed incredible that she had once fit under his arm, that she had been gleeful about eating potato chips, hopping up like a baby seal. He wished Lucy was here, to sit on his other side. They turned toward the flanging lights on the television, the muffled sound of explosion coming into the room.

Underwater Adventure

They Make Love Quietly

She doesn't want to wake Evan, who sleeps in the next room. At six, he's turned fretful, waking at odd hours of the night.

Her husband has been away for weeks, gathering material for a book about Wicca. He's returned with hours of interviews, more material, he says, than he knows what to do with.

She stretches against him, breathing lightly. Sex is always strange after he's been away. They're out of rhythm with each other.

Martin stretches and half sits up, puts his hands behind his head. People always say he's marvelous, so interested in women's issues, so witty and well read.

"I'm bored with you in bed," he says.

She rolls away.

A Planet Party

She plans to drop Evan at the birthday party then do a few errands. She doesn't want to answer questions: "How long have you lived here? What does your husband do? Do you work outside the home?"

She checks the address and pulls up in front of a clapboard house with a deep front porch. Marigolds line the path;

minivans and overturned recycling bins line the street. She doesn't know the little girl, who's in Evan's class. Evan says she's nice, but he says this about everyone.

Evan looks up at her, as if for permission, then presses the doorbell, leaning on it a moment too long. A woman with curly red hair comes to the door and ushers them in. The other children have already arrived, the room filled with humming bodies. Oversized stars, covered with tinfoil and glitter, hang from the chandelier. Star-shaped paper plates shine on the black tablecloth. A chocolate cake, decorated with a sun and planets, rests on the sideboard.

It is perfect. Not annoying, overdone, but done kindly and with heart. The birthday girl, wearing a striped dress with leggings, jumps up and down when Evan hands her his present. His shy grin reveals his pleasure. The girl takes a deep breath and offers Judith some punch; clearly she has rehearsed her manners, and Judith doesn't want to be rude. "I'd love some," she says. Evan hesitates, then steps toward the group.

Bright drawings cover the wall above an upright piano. The house is filled with books and toys piled in plastic bins. They must have other children. Standing next to another mother, she watches the girl's father organize the first game: "Pin the Red Spot on Jupiter." He has a ponytail and beard and narrates each child's blindfolded journey like a carnival barker.

When the games are done, the mother of the birthday girl leads the children down the hall, getting them to take turns washing their hands before sitting down to cake and ice cream.

Judith is filled with the perfection of it: the clutter of plates, the preparations for the day. The husband, looking weary and bemused, comes up behind his wife and whispers something in her ear, presses his mouth into her cloud of red hair.

At Dick Blick's Art Supply

The paintbrushes here are sable and soft. She flicks one, like
a kiss, over her eyelids, cheeks, and lips, the way children
play with makeup. Her own mother wore only lipstick—
tangerine—a gash of misplaced color. Sitting on a shelf,
two truncated hands float on wooden stands—flesh-colored
plastic, without the delicacy of lines. Judith looks at her own
hand: the tiny lines of the first knuckle, the whorl of lines
on the second knuckle like a sapling tree knot. The models
move whichever way she wants. She bends them into odd,
unforgiving poses. A man and woman's right hands. She'd
like to make them touch. They don't fit together quite the
way they should.

No Jews

She's out of step with the culture of the Midwest, the women
with their hot dishes and seasonal sweaters, the silent men,
and finally she realizes what it is: no Jews. Well, there are
some, but she misses certain qualities: conviction, irony, guts.
Everything here is decorousness, smoothing over, smiles.

Evan's first grade teacher takes her aside and says, "Perhaps we can arrange a conference. I want you to know that
I honor your choices, but Evan seems anxious about life at
home these days."

Judith gazes at the teacher's long denim jumper and
clunky shoes, then leans in close.

"Why don't you say what you really mean?"

Solvency

Now, when Martin comes home from a trip, he goes over
the checkbook, the phone bill, the VISA statement. Light
shines out from beneath his study door. Evan is asleep, or

pretending to be. The house is quiet. She reads a novel in the living room.

"What's this?"

With the light at his back, she can't see his expression. She peers at what looks like a credit card statement.

"What?"

"Dick Blick?"

"It's an art supply store."

"Oh, really."

"Really."

"It sounds like a place you'd buy porn."

"Check it out yourself. It's right downtown."

He returns to his study, the click of the door as definitive as a slam.

She Misses the Days of Walter Cronkite

She stopped watching the news when Evan was an infant. Suddenly she felt permeable, as if everything was potentially threatening.

Two towns away, a family starved their thirteen-month-old child to death. The doctor had told them to wean the child from the bottle, so they stopped feeding her. The mother was found not guilty by reason of mental defect. A one-year-old child—so busy, so demanding—how could someone miss a life fading in front of them? Good baby, when it stopped crying. People who leave their children in cars in the summer. They forget! Unbelievable. They must not want to be parents. How could anyone forget a child? The newscast that finally did it was about two brothers in Chicago. A thirteen-year-old dangled his little brother out an eight-story window, then dropped him.

She knows she must leave Martin. It's just a matter of time.

Poetic Justice

Every year, they debate about going to California for Christmas and decide against it. Then they feel sorry for Martin's mother who wants, so badly, to see Evan, and they go. Evan is too young to understand the tension between Martin and his parents, who try to be on good behavior, but every year, at one meal or another, Martin rises from the table, white-faced, furious, and leaves the house for the night.

In early December, the cold has settled into Minnesota. Judith and Evan sit on the living room floor making holiday cards, cutting out snowflakes and decorations. Last night, she and Martin discussed making a donation to Doctors Without Borders and sending their families notes. *A gift has been made in your name.* She imagines making a homemade card and sending it to Martin's father anonymously. She'd use soft construction paper, blunted scissors, glue, and sparkles. She'd give a gift to the United Negro College Fund, especially in his name. He'd open the card while sitting by his pool. He'd be drinking a Lite beer, ranting about Mexicans. *A gift has been made in your name.* The mailing lists he'd be on, the phone solicitations! She giggles to herself, and once she starts to imagine it, she can't stop laughing, the air pressing up through her throat.

"What is it, Mommy? What is it?" Evan laughs simply because she is laughing, thrilled with her burst of humor. She hugs him, smelling the soft child smell of him. When she finally catches her breath, she tells herself that revenge is satisfying only in anticipation, its taste so rare she'd lift the fork and bite the air.

Throwing Like a Girl

When Evan was a toddler, wearing tiny jeans with snaps on the inseams, his blue jeans pulled over the bulk of diapers amused her. At six, he is lithe and coordinated and looks like a growing boy. She pitches the ball to him gently, unsure of its arc. He throws it back to her overhand, the angle of his arm too tight, and standing in the green afternoon, she wants to weep.

"Bring your arm back farther when you throw," she says. "Back farther than your ear."

She throws one overhand, imagining the motion she has seen on television.

He catches it in his mitt. When he throws it back to her, she pushes her hands in front of her, winces, and steps back.

"You don't have to be afraid," he says.

"I know, I just don't have a mitt."

"You can use mine."

"That's okay," she says. "It wouldn't fit."

She can't say that she's afraid he'll learn to throw like her, that now he'll step away from the ball as it comes to him.

"Pitch some to me," he says, picking up his bat.

She tries, but her pitches are inconsistent, some too high, some too low. When he finally hits one, she cheers.

"I'm sorry I'm not better at this," Judith says.

"That's okay," he tells her. "You're good at other things."

Underwater Adventure

Judith suggests doing something as a family and, although they have avoided making this trip before now, Martin agrees to go to the Mall of America to see Legoland.

"I hate even the idea of it," Martin says. "Consumer culture. All that materialistic crap."

"I know, but he's nuts over Legos. It's something we can all do." She tries to keep her tone neutral. Martin will understand the subtext: we can concentrate on Evan; we don't have to talk to each other. "There's an aquarium too." This is her peace offering, which Martin acknowledges with a disgruntled smile.

Evan kneels on the floor, playing with Legos Quality Quidditch Supplies, and because she's already proposed it to Evan, because he wants to go so badly, his silence pains her. He knows he's not supposed to beg.

THEY DRIVE TO Minneapolis on a gray March day, the sky threatening snow. Evan bounces on his seat, anticipating, and when they finally arrive at the mall, park in the vast lot, and walk in the door, she feels stung by the glitter and noise. Evan reaches for her hand.

Martin clenches his jaw as they approach Camp Snoopy, the indoor amusement park. The vast room reaches up three stories and contains a huge Ferris wheel and rides with names like The Timberland Twister and The Kite Eating Tree. A roller coaster rattles over their heads, and Martin looks up.

"Look at that! Do you want to ride on the roller coaster?"

Evan shakes his head and moves next to her.

"You have to try things," Martin says. "You'd like it."

They follow an artificial lane amid the swirling rides, following the signs for Legoland. Whenever she comes to the city, she's aware of the whiteness of their little town. Here, people dress in bright colors; unfamiliar languages swirl around her. Teenagers talk and laugh, flashing braces and cell phones, the girls' pants low on their hips. She is glad they don't have a daughter. She wouldn't know what to tell her.

At first glance, Legoland is simply a toy store, but then Judith sees that everything is made of Legos: a clock tower chiming on the hour, moving dinosaurs, oversized Star Wars figures. Evan scrambles toward a wall of Harry Potter Legos. Dumbledore's Office. Gryffindor Tower! The Remembrall!

"Mom, look at this—the goblins have noses! Legos don't usually have noses." Evan stands in front of a wall of boxes and studies the different scenes.

That morning they told him they would buy him something at the end of the day, and after spending as much time in Legoland as they can stand, Martin finally says, "Come on, Evan. Let's go to the aquarium."

"Can we get something now?"

"After the aquarium, after we've had a ride on the roller coaster."

THE MALL HAS THE USUAL assortment of stores. Even the stores like *Minnesota This 'n' That* are variations on familiar themes; the names and contents could be transposed to Wisconsin or Idaho or Vermont, where they'd sell cheeseheads, potatoes, or maple syrup in leaf-shaped bottles. Of course, there's the inevitability of The Gap, The Museum Store, Lady Foot Locker. Evan tugs them toward the Rainforest Café, where a large mechanical crocodile rests in water. Kids toss coins into his mouth.

"McCaffrey, party of three, your adventure is about to begin," a loudspeaker announces.

"Not the kind of thing you want to hear about a meal, is it?" Martin grins, conspiratorial, and she laughs, feeling her shoulders relax. She remembers when they joked all the time, the brightness between them.

AS THEY STAND IN LINE to buy tickets to the aquarium, beach music floats in from another room. Martin makes waving motions with his arms, doing the crawl, and Evan giggles wildly. Harried mothers holding children, lugging diaper bags and pushing strollers, watch Martin and smile; they must imagine he is like this all the time.

At the entrance to the aquarium there's a simulated forest, a leafy darkness with little pools of water holding different species of turtles. Some turtles blend into their environments; others have bright red and yellow markings. Martin smiles at Evan and imitates a turtle rolling a log. He pretends the log is spinning so fast that the turtle can't keep up. He widens his eyes, waves his fingers, as if they're tiny legs. Evan laughs, and Judith thinks, for a moment, that everything will be all right. She knows Martin feels this is better for Evan; he's learning about the natural world.

At the end of the forest is a tunnel, perhaps ten feet high, surrounded by Plexiglass and water. When they step in, the aquarium is overhead, water surrounding them. It's like a huge MRI machine. They are in the Mississippi River, or an accurate simulation. The catfish, with their oily whiskers, are enormous. "Mis-sis-sippi," "Mis-sis-sippi." Evan whispers the rhythm like a mantra. Martin reads the information about the fish, studies the names, tries to identify the fish swimming past. A large, flat fish glides in front of them, and Judith wishes she could squeeze it, press that dense fleshiness between her palms. As they move further on, to a simulated environment of the Gulf of Mexico, sharks swim above them, their mouths open to reveal three rows of curved teeth. One shark has a small fish swimming directly underneath it.

"Look at that, Evan." She points to a shark curving through the water with a small fish attached to its belly.

An aquarium employee, a slender black man with an African accent, has a microphone pinned to his lapel, and he explains various marine phenomena to the passing crowd.

"That's a remora." His accent is elegant, formal, and she wonders what it must be like to spend all day underwater, embroidering knowledge onto the spontaneous comments of sightseers. "The smaller fish attaches itself to the shark with a piece of tissue that looks like a fin, but actually works as a suction cup."

She nods and smiles. Evan moves up under her hand, leaning against her belly.

Further on, neon fish flit through the tank: turquoise, magenta, tiny bleats of light. Lionfish puff up, their filmy manes waving in the water like bridesmaids in striped chiffon gowns. In a separate tank, an octopus unfurls its tentacles in the inky dark. Up ahead, at the end of the tunnel, there's a gift shop, and another room beyond.

In the final room, children surround a large donut-shaped tank, and the sound of running water fills the room. She looks back toward the tunnel. Martin is still in the aquarium, studying the tropical fish.

"Mom, look, you can touch the fish!" Evan runs up to the tank.

A woman wearing a headset stands on a stepladder above the tank. She explains that the stingrays and small sharks are safe to touch, but their tails are sensitive. And don't move too quickly, she says, the sharks can bite. Judith tries not to make a face. Martin comes up and stands at her shoulder.

"Pull up your sleeves," she says to Evan.

They all lean over the tank, and Evan reaches down toward the stingray. It seems to rise up toward his hand.

"How does it feel?"

"Really soft." His voice is filled with wonder. He reaches down for the small, mottled shark, and she tries not to flinch.

"What does that one feel like?" She keeps her voice even.

"Harder, a little bumpier."

The woman with the headset tells the crowd, "In the tank we have cow-nosed stingrays, and they are quite social."

"Try it, Mom."

She doesn't want to show her hesitation. Martin says she makes Evan too cautious with her fears.

She puts her hand into the cool water and reaches toward the stingray, which rises up to her hand. The stingray is the color of a mushroom, but less firm, unbelievably soft, its skin like wet velvet.

"Oh, that's amazing!" She smiles at Evan, who grins back at her, and she reaches toward the next stingray that comes by.

After they're done, and Martin has taken him to wash his hands, Evan wants to go back to Legoland.

"Please, please, can we go back now?"

She wishes he'd waited to ask. Martin likes to be the dispenser of generosity, not seeming to cede to commercial desires.

"You've got to do more than play Legos," Martin says.

They walk back toward the amusement park. The roller coaster rumbles in the distance.

"One ride on the coaster, and then we'll go back to Legoland," Martin says.

Evan stops and looks up, his lip trembling. Judith sees his understanding: Martin will not back down.

"Okay." Evan's voice is quiet.

"Martin—" She puts her hand on his arm.

He turns, and she is shocked by his fierce expression. His pent-up annoyance has brimmed over into dislike.

"That's not what I was going to say—I was just going to say 'sit in back,' okay?"

Martin puts his hand on Evan's shoulder, pushing him forward. He buys the tickets, and they climb the steps to get in line. The din of talking and laughing and machinery grows loud around her. She stands in the middle of the vast room, watching the roller coaster finish its previous round. Evan meets the height requirement. She tells herself it will be fine.

The cars come to a stop, and the previous group of people get out. Martin steps forward, choosing the car in the front. She feels a thudding in her chest. It will be too much for Evan. She is sick to think that, at six, he already knows the trade-off. To get the Legos, he has to please Martin.

The roller coaster pulls away from the raised station, and the cars begin to clatter around the track. She can't see Evan's face; it goes by too quickly. Parts of the track are hidden by other rides, and for minutes, she can't see Evan at all. At one point, over her head, Martin leans over him, his arm around Evan's shoulders. Evan's mouth is open.

It's over quickly. She's already scouted the place where they'll come out. She moves around a clump of fake trees to get to them, and as she approaches, she sees Martin's pale face, his look of disgust. Evan surges forward, his face crumpled by tears, a large dark mark on the front of his pants, something he hasn't done in years. The time has come; she has to choose. Martin's face is tight with anger as Evan rushes toward her.

Collateral Damage

The stoplight turns yellow and Judith brakes, eyeing the pickup in front of her. A decal in the cab window shows a woman in shorts, bending over; underneath, in script: *Liquor in Front Power in the Rear.* She hopes Evan doesn't ask what it means. At eight, his questions have become harder to answer: What's an X-rated movie? Why did Martin Luther King get shot? What does 'rape' mean?

"I'm getting a pen pal this year," Evan says.

"A new one?"

Last fall, Evan's class had written to Native American kids in northern Arizona. Before Christmas, the class had gathered, then sent, old winter jackets; apparently their pen pals needed them, but Judith found the transaction awkward, as if the cultural exchange culminated in charity. She wondered if Evan hadn't understood completely. He didn't say much about school, which worried her until other mothers told her their boys were the same way; girls, by contrast, seemed always full of news.

"Mrs. Pike says we're going to write letters to soldiers."

"What?"

"Writing letters to Iraq."

Judith hits the turn signal. "What sort of letters are you supposed to write?"

"I don't know."

He makes these announcements just as she drops him off. She parks in a corner of the lot, out of the fray. At the entrance, a rotund girl can't get her cello out of the back of a minivan; mothers double-park in spite of the principal's pleas. Kids on bikes, wearing mushroom-shaped helmets, wobble across the walkways. Every morning, a blonde-haired woman leaves her Ford Expedition running in the NO PARKING zone. Evan stands up in the backseat, leans into the front, and hugs her with his bony arms.

"Can I swing after school?"

"Sure, I'll meet you in back."

He slams the door and runs, pack bouncing on his back, as he dodges through groups of kids and darts in the front door. From a distance, his small dexterities surprise her.

JUDITH IDLES IN THE PARKING LOT, waiting to get out. Around here, it's not politically correct to say so, but she hates the idea of teaching kids to valorize soldiers and, by extension, war. Evan's teacher, Mrs. Pike, is a bland woman who seems more comfortable talking to children than adults. There's probably no harm in the project, but it all seems… trite. And what can a bunch of cards from little kids do for soldiers? Nothing. When she imagines talking to Mrs. Pike, Judith's chest burns. At home, in New York, no one assumes agreement is natural; people thresh out their disagreements, jovially or otherwise, and at least it's clear where people stand. Here in Minnesota, there's the appearance of an agreed-upon norm, which, as she's learned, people don't actually agree on; they're just afraid to make waves. Whenever she questions the status quo, such as the way candy is used as a reward for almost everything, she's given odd looks, and somehow it's said, subtly or directly, that it's never been a problem before, so why is she making a fuss?

Close to the university, she scans the streets for a parking spot. Last month, campaign signs started popping up in people's front lawns. The student rental houses don't have obvious political affiliations, but in the residential neighborhoods, Bush-Cheney or W '04 signs flank Kerry-Edwards signs. In the spring, these neighbors will be hostile but polite. There will be aggressive gardening: beautifully tended flower beds, front walks edged as if precision demonstrates virtue. That's how the adults do it here.

The students are more open. Last year, she started working at the University Counseling Center, a job she hadn't expected to like as much as she does. Before Evan was born, she was a social worker, but when the time came to go back, case work overwhelmed her. Counseling college students, although some have real difficulties, feels more hopeful and, in spite of their youth, she's found a particularly Midwestern quality in the unflinching assessment of their own faults. They don't let themselves off the hook with the moral relativism Martin seems to have mastered.

He has agreed to a separation, but financially, they don't know how they'll manage. Her job helps, which he resents, of course. After they had Evan, it became clear that, even with a baby, her needs were second to Martin's. Evan could be colicky, inconsolable, but Martin had to get one last interview or finish a pitch tape. Granted, he had taken a job in this college town, advising the Communications Department about improving the university radio station. Together they had made the bold move and left New York. They bought a 1920s bungalow because the prices were so low after living in New York. She can hardly believe they have a house with a fenced yard and a rope swing in a tree.

But Martin decided he wasn't cut out for a day job; he missed the rhythm of larger projects.

Now it's hard to imagine moving back to New York. Evan loves living in a house instead of an apartment. He likes his sunlit school and his friends. Freelancing again, Martin is doing a series on election monitoring around the country, and they've come to an agreement: he will travel and use their home as a base; he'll write and call Evan all the time, and hopefully it will sink in gradually that they're splitting up.

AT THE CAFÉ NEAR CAMPUS, the nexus of regulars is as predictable as the cast in a play: a man with a mane of gray hair who chain-smokes outside, a greyhound-like woman with a laptop. The barista, a cheerful young woman, greets Judith: "Double capp?" Two men in jeans and Carhartt jackets, carpenters she imagines, come in together. One of them says something low, almost under his breath, the other nods and smiles, and the first man laughs.

She feels a pang, like hunger. How do you make friends when you're a grown-up? She hasn't figured this out, although there are the obvious answers. People here keep asking if she has a church. *Having* a church, the question makes her laugh, like having a Monopoly piece—a house or a hotel—in her pocket. In the beginning, the town seemed provincial, but then she found some interesting places: the food co-op, a bookstore, a yarn shop. Still, everyone seems to know everyone else.

The local paper has a section called *Neighbors*, and every week, articles describe doctors and dentists who've donated their services in developing countries, ministers with degrees from Yale Divinity School, midwives who've worked in India, glass-blowers, artists, musicians retired from Nashville or major symphonies—so there's evidence of a world beyond the obvious Midwestern doughiness around her. Somehow, she hasn't managed to intersect it.

When Martin is away, she's most aware of her loneliness, but she also feels a vast relief. So much of her energy is spent reading his moods and negotiating their mutual anger. They try to talk while Evan is at school, or at a friend's, so just when it seems she'll have a few hours of quiet, Martin brings up some difficulty, and any potentially peaceful time is spent on

Martin's need to 'process,' which seems endless. Sometimes she simply apologizes for whatever he's upset about, but by now it's become clear that her concessions are merely placating, and Martin is irked about this as well, as if he can't truly win a fight.

SHE WALKS INTO the counseling center and greets Carol, the administrative assistant, who has been here longer than the furniture. Carol's desk and computer are filled with pictures of her grandchildren; the blue backgrounds, shot with pale highlights, show them morphing from little kids with pigtails and big-toothed smiles to adolescents in soccer jerseys and braces.

Judith's office is small, but comfortable enough, decorated with knick-knacks she's taken from home. When they moved, Martin groaned at certain objects, "Oh *that* again, didn't we lose that?" She touches a set of boxes, in graduated sizes, covered in Japanese paper, a purchase that predated her marriage. There was no returning to that time. She would be single again, but different. She turns a Waterford vase to hide a chip; it had belonged to her grandmother, and now it props up a splashy painting by Evan.

Sipping her coffee, she opens her calendar. Some students are relatively uncomplicated. They get drunk and do stupid things, or their parents split up right after they've come to college, and they feel betrayed, understandably, by the abrupt revision of what they thought they knew. Other students are more complex: they have secrets they won't name or eating disorders; the boy wrestlers, the girls with dry skin and hollowed hips, are like knotted strings that may never come undone. The war made complications too. At a state university, close to Fort McCoy, many of the students have boyfriends, girlfriends, or family members being called up. Most of them dread the war; even the students who support it sound worried.

Judith stretches her arms over her head; the muscles below her shoulder blades tighten. She needs movement, nothing so banal as exercise classes, which she hates; she needs a purpose that requires effort. Outside her window, people hurry across campus, their heads down against the wind. Her most genuine interactions are with students, but the conversations are one-sided, as they should be. Sometimes, she wants to tell them how *she* feels, feels the need spilling over in herself, but she refrains. That's not what they've come for. They come for revelation, or insight, or just to get through the day. She sighs. They don't yet know that understanding is just part of it, that understanding a problem doesn't always make it go away.

OVER THE DAY, between students, she thinks of Mrs. Pike. She is younger than Judith—mid-twenties, mid-thirties—it's hard to say. Before confronting her, Judith decides to check the weekly folder that Evan brings home—perhaps there's a note about the pen pal project.

Evan always asks to stay and swing after school, and most days, Judith lets him. In graduate school, Judith had a teacher who believed that rocking chairs soothed patients because the swaying motion mimicked the rhythm of being in the womb while the mother walked. Judith isn't sure about the theory, but she walked a lot when she was pregnant with Evan, all through the Brooklyn neighborhoods they couldn't afford to live in.

DRIVING HOME, she tries to make her questions sound casual.

"So, tell me about your pen pal. Who are you writing to?"

"Someone named Sam."

"What are you going to write about?"

"I don't know."

"I'm sure whatever you write will be fine."

"Mom?"

He prefaces all his questions this way. She's sometimes wants to say, *Just ask it, who else is here?* She checks herself.

"Mom, does John Kerry kill babies?"

She takes her foot off the accelerator. "What?"

"Does John Kerry kill babies to pay for the war?"

"No, sweetheart, of course not. What gave you such an idea?"

"That's what Trevor said."

"He must have misunderstood."

"Alex said it too."

"Who's Alex?"

"His brother. He's in fifth grade."

Judith picks up speed as she gets on the four-lane. Evan doesn't fully understand the mechanics of sex. She can't possibly explain abortion.

"We're having elections at school; we're voting pretend votes, and Trevor said he'd beat Andy up if he voted for Kerry."

"Does your teacher know?" Glancing in the rearview mirror, she sees Evan's calm expectancy. For kids, the most outrageous things in the world seem normal.

"The teachers stay on the blacktop at recess. They don't really notice the kids unless someone's being mean."

Judith tries to give a reassuring smile, but Evan is looking out the window. It seems that all their important conversations take place in the car, with Evan in the backseat, for safety.

THAT NIGHT, after Evan is asleep, she surveys their living room; it is minimalist, almost Japanese in its spareness. Martin doesn't like furniture. She thought he was kidding when he first said it. "What do you mean, you don't like *furniture*?" "I just don't like clutter," Martin said. "It's hard to clean around." Judith wishes for a puffy armchair, melon-colored pillows. Maybe in time, when Martin has a place of his own.

Flawed as he is, Martin can be diplomatic, and she wishes he were here now. His manipulative abilities are various: he can take a tiny comment and blow it up into polarizing difficulty, but he can also see what's good or useful in a bad situation by turning it to the side, holding it in a different light. Deft in conflict, he can find a patch of common ground and work from there. Martin would let Evan know that his teacher had misstepped, but he'd say it in way that would allow Evan to be comfortable at school.

When the phone rings, she grabs it before the second ring.

"What's wrong?" Martin sounds bored.

She explains what Evan has told her about his soldier pen pal, and about the kid in his class threatening other kids over the pretend election.

Martin laughs.

"What's so funny?"

"It's not funny, really. They try so hard to be politically correct, but then they trod on people this way. You should talk to Mrs. Pike."

"She's obtuse. There was nothing in their folders about it. I'll spell it all out for her, and she still won't really get it that some parents might not like their kids writing to soldiers."

"I know. But it's fair for you to ask her to give the kids some options. And let her deal with the parents of the bully. That's her job."

"Okay," Judith says. "Thanks for calling back." It feels odd to be formal with him, but she doesn't know how to end this. "I've got to go, I'm really beat."

DRIVING EVAN TO SCHOOL the next morning, she says, "Mrs. Pike is nice to think of this project of writing to the soldiers. They're doing what they think is right, but she should have asked the parents how they felt about it first."

"She said the soldiers are hot and tired and need cheering up."

"I bet they do."

"We're supposed to buy them wipes too."

"Wipes?"

"Baby wipes. They get sand on their faces."

"We can get some at Target."

Usually, Judith drops Evan off, but this morning she parks. At the entrance, she smiles at the mother of a boy Evan has played with a few times, but the woman is looking the other way, toward a friend who walks over and hugs her. She clutches her friend's arm. Clearly, there's a problem, but Judith doesn't know her well enough to intrude and ask what she can do. She follows Evan down the hall and, while Evan is stowing his coat in his cubby, she walks into the classroom. An aquarium fills one corner; kids mill around the room.

The classroom aide is at the door, welcoming the children, checking to see whether they need hot lunch. At the front of the room, a woman writes on the board.

"Is Mrs. Pike here today?"

"I'm sorry, she's not. She called in sick."

"Do you think she'll be in tomorrow?"

"I hope so."

Judith kisses Evan goodbye, then walks down the hallway filled with bright coats and boots.

WHEN JUDITH GETS in her car and turns the key, the engine makes a clicking sound but doesn't start. She sits back, furious, and presses her palms against her eyes. She can call a tow truck, but who can she call for a lift? No one.

An orange light on the dashboard glows. Oh! Neutral. Judith puts the car in park, turns the key, and it starts.

What is wrong with her? She wants to put her head on the steering wheel and weep. Instead, she backs out of her parking space and, moving forward, sees the principal, in a scarlet vest, waving stragglers in the door.

Judith knows she has failed. When you're young, complaining about a bad boyfriend is simply evidence that you have one, but admitting to a bad marriage is a whole other category. It isn't so simple as the fact they've grown apart, or that Martin has put his work first; she's ashamed to admit the truth: she married Martin knowing he could be manipulative, even a little mean at times, but she imagined she was special to him, that his calculations wouldn't be directed at her. How foolish she'd been, arrogant really.

Once, when Evan was about a year old, she told Martin that she was too tired to have sex, and Martin said, *You're stingy with your emotions. You withhold yourself until you're sure of your position. No wonder you like social work. You sit in judgment on people, write reports about whether they get to keep their kids or not. What makes you think you have the right to judge? You're an emotional miser.*

She'd thought of herself as shy.

Stingy seems harsh; perhaps she is judgmental, but most people can be at times. She was raised to be decisive—her father didn't want a ditzy girl—but it was mean of Martin to make the connection to her work. She had hated recommending kids for foster care—the system was a mess—but what did you do about a mother who left kids locked in an unheated apartment for days? Boyfriends who pimped out their girlfriends' kids?

She'd attributed her bashfulness to being an only child. She'd never had a crowd of friends, never thrown herself into friendships, or love affairs, unless she knew she'd be received with affection.

THE FOLLOWING DAY, Judith goes into the school again. At the front of the classroom, Mrs. Pike arranges models of geometric shapes. She wears a dress with duck-shaped pockets, like a nursery school teacher, and up close, she seems younger than her lumpy shape suggests. Is she pregnant? Hard to say, but of course it's better not to ask.

"Can we talk after school?" Judith asks.

Mrs. Pike looks up, her expression surprised. "Of course, if you have any concerns, I'm happy to talk to you."

"It's not about Evan. It's about your latest pen pal project. I think you should have checked with parents about the appropriateness of it."

Mrs. Pike tightens her lips.

"Having kids write to soldiers implies they support the war. Not everyone does."

"But the soldiers need our support."

"Of course, but I don't think that co-opting a bunch of third-graders is good for them."

The children begin to stream into to the classroom.

"I'm happy to discuss this later." Mrs. Pike's chapped lips are prim.

OVER THE DAY, Judith silently rehearses what she'll say. Her eleven o'clock patient, a pale girl with violet fingernails, says "like" between every word, and after a few minutes, Judith can hardly stand it. She wishes she could call Kaiya, in New York, for a reality check, but there's no time. Sometimes, at night, when she calls a friend from home, Evan wakes up to use the bathroom and asks who she's talking to. Once, she said 'Daddy' when she'd really been talking to Kaiya. Evan said, "You don't sound like that when you talk to Daddy."

WHEN SHE ARRIVES that afternoon, Evan is waiting out front, and Judith tells him he can swing until she comes out. Walking towards his classroom, her pulse throbs in her neck.

"Please have a seat," Mrs. Pike says. Her skin is puffy at the corners of her eyes, a rash that looks like eczema. She gestures to one of the little chairs, as if she and Judith might sit down cozily together, knees under their chins.

"I'll stand," Judith says. "I don't know how much there is to say. I wish you'd checked with parents before proposing that students write to soldiers."

Standing behind the models of geometric shapes, Mrs. Pike grasps a red octagon. "Some of our students have parents who are serving. Writing letters makes them feel connected."

"Lots of parents oppose the war, and their opinions deserve to be respected as well."

"Well, we've already started the project, so I don't know what I can do." Mrs. Pike pushes out her bottom lip.

Judith tries not to focus on a blackhead on Mrs. Pike's cheek. Wouldn't she notice it looking in the mirror? Brushing her teeth?

"We can take it up with the principal then," Judith says. "I'm sure you ran your idea by him. I'm happy to take it right up to the superintendent if I have to." Judith gazes at her and waits, a technique she learned from Martin. Silence makes people uncomfortable if you look them in the eye.

"There's nothing wrong with supporting our troops." Mrs. Pike looks away and shifts a red cone, seemingly unaware of her hand, like a street vendor doing a sleight of hand trick.

"Of course not. I just object to the blanket endorsement. These kids aren't old enough to understand our political climate."

"My sister's in Iraq," Mrs. Pike says. She sinks into a chair and studies the backs of her hands. Her fingernails are short, bitten down like a girl's. When she turns to look up, her face round and unsure, Judith suddenly sees her like a child in a sunflower costume, her face ringed by yellow petals. It's so clearly unreal that Judith shakes her head, then realizes it must seem that she's denying what Mrs. Pike is saying.

"My sister joined the Army to help pay for college. She never planned on a war; she just wants to be a nurse."

Judith blinks, and the sunflower petals dissolve. She's learned you can tell people the truth, but if they don't want to hear it, it doesn't make any difference. All those movies where a righteous character delivers a speech that changes people's minds—life simply doesn't work like that. Judith stifles her first urge, to reassure her, then says, "Maybe you can offer students the option of writing to nurses or medical personnel, not just to soldiers."

Mrs. Pike looks down at her lap.

More softly, Judith says, "On a different topic, but I'm afraid it's related, Evan tells me that one of the kids in your class has been bullying other kids about these school elections. Apparently, someone named Trevor has been telling his classmates that Kerry kills babies to pay for the war."

Mrs. Pike looks up, her mouth open.

"Is there someone named Trevor in your class?"

"Yes."

"Well, that's what he's been telling the other kids. Apparently, he's got a brother named Alex who's saying it too."

"That's not right."

"Well, obviously, but what are you going to do about it?"

"Do?"

Judith tries not to sound exasperated. "Look, if you set up these sort of learning experiences, like school elections, you have to deal with the results."

"We don't teach Sex Ed in Health until fifth grade. I'm sure they don't talk about abortion."

"That's not what I'm saying. You need to speak to the kid's parents, or the principal needs to talk to them. You can't have the students bullying each other about how they vote in an elementary school election. Isn't that what the whole war is supposed to be about? Creating democracy? Allowing people to vote without being threatened?"

"Their mother is head of the PTA."

Judith raises her hands, palms upward.

Mrs. Pike looks bewildered, as if Judith has sped through a math problem and is impatient that other people can't follow her explanation. "I'll talk to the principal," Mrs. Pike says. She looks beaten, as if all she wants to do is go home and have a good cry.

THE FOLLOWING DAY, Judith waits for Evan after school. She gathers with the other parents, mostly mothers, although a few fathers, college students, and babysitters routinely gather in front, waiting for the kids to be released. She doesn't really want to continue the conversation with Mrs. Pike, but it seems unavoidable.

Evan comes out holding a large, floppy drawing. "Can I swing for a little while?"

"Sure, what's this?"

"Civilization timeline!" He shouts, gleeful, then pushes it off to her and turns, heading for the swings.

She rolls up the paper, catching a glimpse of the pyramids, which he's colored a deep orange. "I'll put this in the car, but then I need to go inside for a minute. I'll be out back in a little bit."

Evan grins and disappears through the playground gate. His emotions are still so pure. She can't remember feeling so single-minded about anything. Martin maybe, when they first met, but look how that turned out.

She sets the timeline and Evan's backpack in the car. The rise and fall of civilizations. She smiles. As a kid, she had wished for a huge timeline that filled the wall of the classroom. Together, they'll look at Evan's when they get home. She crosses the parking lot and weaves through the crowd still waiting by the front door.

The afterschool kids are digging in their cubbies, burrowing into the lost and found box, shouting and charging down the hall. She takes a deep breath and walks into Evan's classroom. Mrs. Pike is standing in front, talking to another mother. The teacher is wearing pants and a turtleneck sweater and seems more grown up than before.

"I can come back," Judith says.

Mrs. Pike looks over, "We're just finishing up, if you can wait."

The mother murmurs something, then laughs. She glances at Judith on the way out.

Mrs. Pike sits down and gestures toward a chair near her. Judith takes a seat.

"I talked to the principal." Mrs. Pike looks at a point just beyond Judith's shoulder. "He's going to talk to Trevor and Alex's mother—I just can't deal with her." Then Mrs. Pike looks directly at Judith and takes a trembling breath. "I don't think I can do this anymore."

"Do what?"

"Teach."

Judith studies her, trying to see if she is serious or merely wrought up. Mrs. Pike's eyes are reddened with fatigue or allergies or tears. "Something like this is no reason to stop teaching," Judith says.

"I think it is. I can't take this." Mrs. Pike gestures at the air between them, flipping her hand back and forth as if she were shooing Judith away. "I like the kids, which everyone warned me was the tiring part, but I don't think I'm really a good *teacher*. All I know how to do is to be encouraging. I don't have…." She looks up, and Judith feels her difficulty, as if the gears of her thought are stuck in something gluey. "I'm not an analytical person. I didn't think about the politics of writing the letters. I was just trying to make people feel better."

"But that's a wonderful quality—you shouldn't feel bad about that."

"It's not so wonderful, obviously, because it's gotten me into this mess."

"It's not such a mess, is it? The principal isn't upset is he?"

"No, he's great, really. I just… I don't think I can keep doing this because everything I do is going to be… I don't know. I'll keep wondering if there's some whole part I hadn't thought of." Tears well up in her eyes. "All I know how to do is to be nice, to encourage people. I mean, in high school I was a *cheerleader*. I *loved* it. Isn't that pathetic?" Mrs. Pike puts her face into her hands and muffles a sob.

Judith slides her chair over the linoleum, reaches over and puts a hand on Mrs. Pike's back. She pats her for a moment, then rubs in circles, the way she would for a child who can't settle. What in the world has she done? What a schmuck she's been, using Martin's tactics on this poor woman. "It's not pathetic at all. I did mean what I said about the political aspect of this, but I certainly didn't mean to make you this doubtful. Believe me, you have no idea what a rare thing it is to encourage people. Practically everyone does the opposite, automatically. Constantly, really."

"I feel like going home and crawling into bed and pretending the rest of the world isn't going on."

"We all feel that way sometimes."

"I feel that way a lot."

"Me too," Judith says.

Mrs. Pike sits up, takes a tissue out of her pocket, and blows her nose loudly.

"Look," Judith says. "I did need to say what I thought, but I don't want you to worry about this. You absolutely should keep teaching. So, a little misstep. So what? Evan loves coming here, and he loves your class. You know that, don't you?"

Mrs. Pike's expression brightens. "He does, doesn't he?"

"Yes. And selfishly, I really want him to feel happy and stable somewhere because…" Judith hesitates, "*Please* don't say anything to Evan, or anyone else for that matter, but his father and I are separating. We've been in that process for a little while. My husband doesn't like it here, and he travels for work now, but Evan loves living here, and I just can't imagine moving him now."

Mrs. Pike's expression moves from dismay to surprise. "I could tell by your accent you're from somewhere else."

"New York."

"Do you have friends here? People who will help you out?"

"No," Judith says. "I don't really." And she is horrified to feel tears starting in her throat. She takes a deep breath.

Mrs. Pike regards her gravely. "I've lived in Minnesota or Wisconsin my whole life, but there are lots of people like you around here—people who come from the Cities, or who move here from somewhere else. They're kind of a different crowd."

"I never really had a crowd."

"You'll find them. Sometimes it just takes a little time."

Judith nods and gathers her coat. "Really, I mean it. Please don't quit doing this. We all need you."

Mrs. Pike smiles shyly.

Judith walks out, down the hallway, which is quiet now, and takes a door that will let her out onto the playground. Evan is swinging, laughing with a boy Judith doesn't know. For a minute, the boys are swinging together, almost in unison, then Evan kicks his legs out harder, and they begin to arc at different rates.

"Mom, do an underdog," Evan calls.

"You're too big!" Judith smiles.

"Oh, come on!" Evan wiggles his legs as if he's doing a flutter kick.

"Once!" Judith laughs. She jogs around to the back of the swings. Her legs and breasts feel heavy, as if the water of her body has settled in them. She pauses, measuring the rhythm of Evan's rise and fall through the air, then runs toward him, pushing forward and through, ducking. Evan's sneaker grazes her head. "Ow!" Grinning, she brushes a piece of mulch out of her hair, then stands, breathing hard, hands on her hips. The boys laugh, swinging forward and back in the bright October air.

She can't believe Mrs. Pike is the first person she has told about Martin. Judith feels as if she's let something go. Let Martin go. She will stay. She will buy some comfortable furniture for the house. Maybe she can find someone who'll go shopping with her, someone with a kid Evan's age. They could all drive up to the Cities and go to Ikea. How banal. Frivolous. It might be fun. From the edge of the playground, she hears the sound of someone calling. A mother waves in the distance. Judith looks to the other boy to see if he hears.

"Are you Ben?" she asks, "I think your mother is calling you."

He looks up to see, then hops off the swing as it arcs outward. He grabs his pack, shouts "Bye, Evan!" over his shoulder, and takes off towards the parking lot. The mother gives a little wave, as if to say 'thanks,' and Judith lifts her hand in response.

II

Listeners at the Still Point

Francoise stood in front of her mother's picture window, tracing Toronto's skyline with her finger. The skyscrapers around the Lakeshore, usually bright and metallic, were discolored by a pale scrim of heat. She slid her finger up against the tower's slender tip; its spire didn't pierce the atmosphere. "I don't see why I need to ask Ira's permission. I just want to get out of the city in August," Francoise made her voice sound reasonable. She knew what her mother was afraid of; she wanted to make her say it.

Diane stretched out on the sofa, studying a cookbook filled with glossy photographs. She held a place with one finger and flipped back and forth between the pictures. Swaddled in the sofa's round arms and scalloped back, she seemed to be resting in a bulky vanilla cloud.

"But it's so remote there, what will you do?"

"I'll bring some charcoals and some paints," Francoise said.

"We'll discuss it after your appointment on Tuesday," Diane said. She had used the same tone when Francoise was five, when her father was still with them.

"You rely on him for everything."

"Francoise, that's not true."

Francoise twisted a strand of hair around her finger. Her therapist had become a foreign and annoying fixture in her life; like a scratch on a pair of glasses, he imposed himself on her vision like a tiny distracting fleck. She could be running errands, or listening to music, when one of his comments, quiet as a raised eyebrow, flitted through her thoughts. From the beginning he wanted her to call him Ira, instead of Dr. Abrams, as if this familiarity would encourage her to be more talkative. Diane occasionally consulted with him, but she and Francoise never saw him together. It was as if, for a few hours a week, her mother had hired a substitute husband.

"You could come with me. It would be a break for both of us," Francoise suggested.

"I have too much to do before this shoot. I have to find half a dozen things." Diane marked a place in her book then closed it. Her work as a photo-stylist bled into their daily life, and she moved through the world leaving elegant gestures in her wake: flowers in the bedroom, leftovers served in special dishes, cloth napkins. Not merely fastidious, her mother had a way of pulling unusual things together and making them fit, the ability to make what might be whimsical, whole. She had stumbled on this métier after her husband left. Disappeared in fact, a few postcards from the western provinces, then nothing. Why had he left? That was what Francoise had never understood. Over the years, when she had asked, her mother had pursed her lips and bowed her head, as if the reason was too unbearable to name.

She remembered her mother sitting in the evenings over the checkbook, touching the calculator keys with a pencil eraser. The light from a small desk lamp shone on her hair. Francoise had believed that she did this over and over because the figures, if pursued, might come out differently. Diane had eventually talked her way into a job in advertising, and in a decade of generous budgets, she had become sought out. Her taste, people said, was impeccable.

"I'm going out for a bit." Francoise turned away from the window. The wide brightness was oppressive; the apartment seemed too close to the humid sky.

AS SOON AS SHE STEPPED out of the lobby, she paused to light a cigarette. She didn't smoke in front of her mother, who would interpret it as a sign of anxiety. Store windows mirrored her as she strolled down the street. She had her mother's coloring—olive skin, light brown hair, a thick tangle falling halfway down her back. The contrived wildness made her angular face seem delicate. She did not think of herself as pretty: she had a small, square chin, a once-broken nose, deep-set hazel eyes. An envious friend once said she would have made a beautiful young man. A birthmark, a soft brown comma, splashed the side of her right cheekbone and ran down into her cheek. When she was little, her father had explained that everyone had some tiny imperfection: he said God had smudged her with his thumb because she was so pretty.

In the heat, the wide sidewalk felt soft under her sneakers, like the thick rugs in Ira's office. He had been recommended to Diane almost six years ago, after Francoise was expelled from university. She had always been moody—temperamental, Diane had called it—but in the springtime of her sophomore year Francoise had slipped over an invisible border, invisible because most of the time, really, she felt fine. After 'the incident,' as Diane referred to it, they had pressed Francoise to talk about it, but she had never adequately been able to explain how the pressure of thinking about something so many different ways, the containment of so many perspectives, built up inside her head until it became colors and shapes, hard and bright, intersecting, until it was all too much, and her thoughts went white, like chalk-line drawings against a dark blue board. It happened so quickly, and then the world outside snapped back, bright and unreal, its focus too sharp, like coming out of a movie in daytime. Ira made notes of what she said and multiplied them, spinning her words into something apart from her, until she didn't want to talk to him at all. It was talking about it—being forced to put into words what wasn't meant to be voiced—that had blown things out of proportion. Shortly after her twenty-fourth birthday, Ira and her mother agreed she must take medication. Francoise hated the way it made her feel—drowsy, muffled, as if her thoughts were wrapped in cotton. The pills seemed to prevent the buildup of pressure, but they also blunted the ends of her perception, as if the subtle shadings in a palette had been removed, and what remained was plain and bright, mediocre. Painting, even drawing, seemed to require too much energy. She couldn't imagine going through her life feeling so sleepy and vague.

AT HER APPOINTMENT THAT WEEK, Francoise waited until almost forty minutes had passed before she made her case for going on vacation.

"It's my uncle's summer house; he's a priest in Quebec. Every year he sends us cards at Christmas and Easter, and offers us the cottage for a few weeks. My mother won't even consider it."

"Why is that?"

"He's my father's brother."

"Why do you think he offers it?"

Francoise squinted at the white light beyond the venetian blinds.

"I think, maybe, he feels bad about my father leaving. It's a way of making up, well, he can't make it up, but... I wonder if he knows where my father is. Or what's happened to him." She lowered her voice and tried to sound encouraging. "He's sent us pictures, it looks lovely, a little place on Tancook Island, off the south coast of Nova Scotia."

"Why do you want to go?"

She blew out of her mouth, exasperated. "I want to get out of this awful heat, have a change of scene. I could do some sketching, bring some watercolors. It would be good for me." She closed her eyes and imagined that, instead of his inevitable brown suit and argyle socks, he wore loose, white clothes, a white turban over his dark hair. He would gaze at her with compassion, let her out of this stifling city. The antique clock on his cabinet ticked. She wanted to smash it. "I'm feeling good these days, I'll take my medicine." The phrase echoed, *take my medicine*, as if it were a punishment, as if it were her fault that voices talked to her, as if she wanted them.

The air conditioner grew loud in the silence.

"I don't see any reason why you shouldn't. I think this heat is awful myself."

Francoise rewarded him with a smile. He smiled back; his teeth were small, his smile genuine in the defenseless way of men. She tried not to rush out the door.

ON THE WAY HOME, she bought a fresh sketchpad.

"Ira says I can go!" Francoise shouted as she bounced in the door. Diane sat on the living room floor, surrounded by swatches of fabric, linen napkins and lacquered chop-sticks. The room was still. Francoise closed the door behind her gently.

"What are you working on?"

"I'm doing an ad for a Japanese restaurant downtown." Diane shook out a batik napkin and set a small bamboo tray against it. She stared at them for a moment, then looked up at Francoise. "So, he really thinks it's all right?"

"Yes, he does." She hated how her mother relied on Ira to decide whether her thoughts were in or out of bounds. The idea of lines, of neat delineation, seemed to comfort her mother, who saw everything as a sign of going up or coming down. But that wasn't it at all: it was tiresome, how little her mother understood. Sometimes, Francoise had a sense of shifting sideways, picking up speed, and often the feeling receded. Other times her thoughts came quickly, moving her into new alcoves in her mind that opened out, one onto the other, like a long series of hidden rooms. She was arriving at her secret self, a place still and perfect. She saw images of what she would paint: fantastic cities floating in violet, surrounded by moats and canals, linked by turning bridges.

Last year she had found a stack of books hidden in Diane's nightstand. Francoise read them while her mother was at work and saw how everything was screened through a medical vocabulary. The books were highlighted with a thick marker, and Francoise felt a sting of recognition at certain sections marked with clear yellow, but some passages had nothing to do with her at all, and she felt angry that her mother was clutching at books to categorize her. She understood her mother was frightened, and theories were something her mother could grasp. No one else could hear the voices. The medication kept them quiet, but it also made her cotton-mouthed and listless. Every time she took her pills, she felt she was being unfaithful to herself in a small but significant way, like smoking a cigarette when she was trying to quit. Francoise had tried to tell her how seldom the voices came, but her mother had looked nervous and changed the subject.

Ira had probably told Diane the less said the better. He had told Francoise not to name the voices, that it would give them weight, but each of the three voices was distinct. The first voice, high and playful, was mischievous, like a child who poses questions to test an adult's patience. The second was comforting, a voice of good counsel. All of them were oddly sexless, but the second voice made her think of a wise, older woman. The third couldn't properly be called a voice—it didn't speak—but it was darkly liquid, fearful. She knew it rather than heard it, felt its apprehensive presence tinge her thoughts like spilled ink.

They began her freshman year at university, layering her anxiety about school with questions of their own. Little questions and phrases, like whispered fragments in an empty room. She told herself they weren't real. Hearing voices was what happened to crazy people. Sometimes they were dormant for months at a time; sometimes she was sure it had all been a phase. They might never come back.

THROUGH THE PLANE WINDOW, Lake Ontario dropped away below her. Toronto was dulled by a filmy wave of heat. She had expected to feel pleasure at her escape, but her medication made her feel lethargic and bored. This week would be her test. She would see for herself. She settled back in her seat and wondered about her uncle. He had been so courteously persistent in offering the cottage; he must feel sorry for them. As a child, she hadn't believed he was truly her father's brother; his collar made him seem a kind of foreigner, a man with black-framed glasses and flowing robes. She did see a resemblance when they laughed. Once, when her uncle was visiting, her father twisted a lemon over a shallow glass bowl in the kitchen; he poured a little honey in the lemon rind and handed it to her. Sweet and sour pinched her mouth. He barked "whiskey sour!" in a funny voice, and the room spun with laughter. A few simple words towards the end of a meal made the brothers roar, slap the table, and Francoise remembered her mother smiling too, and then she herself started to laugh without knowing why and a buoyant light filled her and rippled out across the room.

Even then, her uncle had a busy parish in Quebec. Why had he bought a cottage in Nova Scotia? When she wrote to ask him about staying there, he answered quickly, saying how delighted he'd be to have her use it. A neighbor had the key and would be expecting her.

Finally, she would do some painting. Already Francoise felt it, like the tingle before a headache. When she was small, her mother had bragged about her drawing ability; as Francoise grew older, her art teachers commented on her feel for line and color. Now, Diane saw her painting as an omen of trouble. Rather than upset her mother and risk further containment, Francoise mostly left her colors alone.

As the plane began its descent into Halifax, they circled over a bright splattering of lakes and dark pine forests split by slim roads. In the airport, the car rental counter was easy to find, and she studied the map on her phone while the agent checked her credit card. The ferry for Tancook Island left from Chester, an hour's drive.

Chester was a village of white clapboard houses and neatly tended hedges. She parked and walked past a few bed-and-breakfasts, a bakery, and several shops that sold handmade tourist gifts: gingham pot holders and hand-sewn children's toys. A banner announcing *Race Week* stretched across Main Street, and posters with a pen and ink drawing of a sloop filled the shop windows. It had been ages since she'd been anywhere unfamiliar. The town felt manicured, best foot forward, like a child in church clothes, but the air felt clear and cool. At a little drug store, she picked up a ferry schedule and asked where she could buy groceries. Her uncle had said she should buy food in Chester; the island market sold only canned food and dry goods.

She lugged her bag and groceries down the wharf. The harbor, ringed with pines and few clapboard warehouses, was quiet; a forest of pale masts stood out against the trees. From the boats, the sounds of a small radio, slapping water, and fragments of conversation floated through the air. She stopped and shifted the bag of groceries to her other arm. At the end of the dock, a bearded man in a blue uniform coat and old jeans issued tickets and guided people onto the ferry. She paid him and saw that he noted her, a stranger, as he told her to watch her step.

Inside the boat, the passengers sat in clusters on molded plastic benches. She sat down near three white-haired ladies, two of them gently teasing a third about her youthful figure. The slender one tapped her knee with her hand, *oh go on with you now, I don't,* she protested. They nodded at Francoise and smiled. She arranged her bags on the bench seat and went up on deck.

On the dock, two men fastened cables to a large refrigerator box. The winch creaked as they signaled for the box to be lifted, and it tilted into the air, swaying toward the boat. A pile of supplies mounded on the dock—kerosene, mail, a blue armchair covered in plastic.

When the motors shifted and the boat started to pull away, she walked to the prow and looked out toward the ocean. Sails glided on the horizon, the indigo water like new paint mixed with only a single drop of water. She stood, feeling the sun on her face, the cool air, the call of silence; then she went below deck and rummaged through her bag, feeling for her prescription bottle. Cupping it in her palm, she returned to the deck. As they picked up speed, she leaned over the rail and stared down into the water, pale green and white where the boat cut it. She knew what was inside her head and what was outside it. That was the important thing. You didn't go through your whole life being fine, and then all of a sudden go crazy. Everyone had contradictory impulses. It was just that in her, these disparate urges had coalesced into distinct voices. The medication had been a mistake; it dulled everything and made her feel quiet, unconnected to the world. She opened her hand and watched a pale dot fall into the water, then she tipped the container and a scattering of dots fell into the spray.

When she looked up, a red-faced man was staring at her. She blushed and looked away. From where he stood, he couldn't have seen the flight of tiny pills, but her thoughts seemed loud, as if they'd been spoken. She hoped she hadn't been moving her lips in thought. When the ferry cut its engines and eased into the dock, he disappeared.

BRIGHT HOUSES STUDDED the land surrounding the harbor: turquoise, raspberry; she'd never seen houses painted such colors. Her uncle had sent pictures of his cottage so she could find it—there were no house numbers on the island; there was only one road. She pulled out her phone. He'd told her to turn left at the end of the jetty and walk about a quarter of a mile. He'd drawn a little map that showed the road running along the north side of the island, splitting into a fork on the east; one branch leading to the market, the other to a beach. The road didn't even make a complete loop; the island's south side was rocky beachfront. She picked up her packages and started down the gravel road. To her left, the ocean stretched in a vast gray breadth. By the roadside, cornflowers, black-eyed Susans, and tiny scarlet-petaled stars bloomed in the sun. Inland, the countryside appeared forested and hilly.

Her arms were tired; she sweated through her t-shirt. Ahead, a small gray clapboard house matched the photos. She set down her bags and groceries on the porch and went across the road to get the key. Before she knocked, a round-faced woman in a plastic apron that said *Bar B-Q* came to the door.

"Hello, dear. Father Austin told us you'd be coming. You're a painter, he says." Her expression was curious. "I turned on the furnace, so you'd have hot water and some heat at night." She turned back toward the kitchen and yelled, "Harmon, fetch the key, will you?"

A long-haired boy wearing an Iron Maiden t-shirt appeared behind her. He pushed the key at Francoise, staring at a point beyond her shoulder. She didn't think she should linger, so she thanked them and walked back across the road. Her belongings and groceries on the porch seemed vibrant, out of place next to the shuttered windows and weathered paint.

When she let herself into the house and shut the door, the sound of the ocean was cut off, and the silence seemed rich, like the opening shot of an old movie that reveals a room before the action starts. The living room was furnished with comfortable armchairs, a striped love seat, white ceramic lamps on pale wood tables. It wasn't rustic, or masculine as she had expected. There were no photos or pictures—only a few old paperbacks, probably left by another visitor, scattered on bare bookshelves by the television. A large mirror hung on one wall. She'd hoped for some image of her father among her uncle's things. In the bedrooms, she opened the dresser drawers: each was neatly lined with shelf paper, clean and unoccupied. She found a package of tissues, a Tom Clancy novel, not one photo or scrap of handwritten paper. The absence of sound was palpable, pressing on her ears. When she turned on the refrigerator, its hum rippled the silence.

The living room was light, uncluttered, a perfect place to work if she had to paint indoors. The pleasant anonymity of the room seemed sad though. She lit a cigarette. Her mother wouldn't talk about it, but Francoise remembered coming home from school one day and knowing that her father had left. She went into her parents' bedroom to look for what he might have left behind. The large bed was made; the room seemed diminished. She stepped into her father's side of the closet and, standing amidst his suits, she breathed his cologne and felt the scratchy wool and linen against her cheeks. She sat down on the low shelf that held his shoes and leaned against the wall, looking up at the dark suits, the empty arms reaching down to her like the soft arms of ghosts.

THE FOLLOWING DAY she felt lighter. She walked, she napped; it was so nice to be alone and do as she pleased. If she could stay here and paint, and the voices did not come, then it meant she was all right. It was foolish to spend her whole life taking a drug to keep them away.

She felt shy, at first, about choosing a place to paint. Every person on the island—there were only forty or fifty inhabitants—seemed aware of her arrival. The first day, she set up an easel in the front yard. The long grass blew around the boundary fences like a Wyeth painting in bright colors, and the trees swayed and settled as if breathing. Over the road, and the few widely spaced houses beyond, the azure ocean glistened.

She had brought watercolors because they were easier to carry, but after so long, what if nothing she did pleased her? The lush grass and the sea, the tiny, scarlet flowers clustered by the fence invited her, and she wanted to put their brightness into something of her own making. She dampened her brush and paused over the paints. When she touched her brush to the paper, a ripple of connection: paint, water, paper, dipping her brush the way her small hand had reached for holy water in church; her father teaching her to cross herself: *Father, Son, Holy Ghost*. She swept a wash of blue against the paper and felt the breeze washing over her.

That night she felt festive. She sautéed scallops in butter in a cast iron pan. The thick rounds of fish grew firm in the heat, and she drank a glass of wine with her dinner and thought how good it was to be coming back to herself. After dinner she sat and smoked. She tried to read one of the paperbacks that someone had left, but the book didn't occupy her, and she stretched out on the sofa and thought about how glad she was to be away, how everyone had made too much of just one incident, something that was mostly a temper tantrum on her part.

In April, her sophomore year at university, she had gone to the art studio to decide which paintings to submit for her class portfolio. Late in the afternoon, the light on the granite buildings faded from violet to gray. She pulled out her stack of watercolors and set them on an empty table in the middle of the studio. Moving slowly through the stack, she studied each painting, then slid it over to a separate pile. Her earliest work was on the bottom, and some paintings seemed almost unfamiliar. She had thought of each one as a separate piece, but reviewing them together, she saw how they revealed her. It was like seeing a friend with her siblings for the first time: the shadow or impulse of a gesture arose from the same place. Most of the paintings were imaginary cityscapes. Fantastic buildings floated above the ground or hovered in odd juxtapositions. Tiny figures walked through doors turned sideways. The colors—orange, magenta, vermilion—were bold, or that was what she'd intended, but now they seemed ugly, like clown faces gone evil.

Shadows settled in the tiled corners. She moved to turn on the lights, then stopped. She didn't want to see anymore; it disturbed her, how her paintings revealed the kaleidoscopic garishness inside her.

Then the first voice, a high, wispy laughter, seemed a beating glimmer in her ear. The voice had flickered at the edge of her consciousness for months, and she thought of it as playful, a daring part of herself. She lit a cigarette and saw herself touching a match to the corner of a painting. *Touch it. Just touch it.* The first voice was always light, urging her to touch, to try. *Touch it. Go on.* The whimsy of the idea pleased her. Then the second voice, a voice that often soothed her or encouraged her, the voice she desired, said, *yes, go on,* steady and comforting, as if she could take care of something disagreeable, but necessary.

She pulled a painting from the stack and struck a match. The light flared up from her fingers and the black line moved down the match stem. She held it. Then she lit another and, lowering her hand, touched it to the corner of the painting. It wouldn't catch at first, so she struck another match and held it to the paper until a small orange flame spread across the corner in an uneven, widening line. She touched another match to a reluctant stretch of paper and the painting flared up, drowning the colors into dark ash. Then she did another and another.

Later, she tried to explain that she didn't feel commanded; she wasn't doing anything in spite of herself, but when she revealed the voices, her mother's reaction frightened her more than what she'd done.

The next day Francoise decided to look for a different spot to paint. She had already followed the road to the east where it forked: one way led to a ramshackle market with a rusted gas pump, the other to a little schoolhouse. Walking down the road in the other direction, she passed houses with vegetable gardens and clothes hanging out to dry. The pavement ended at the edge of a large field; tire tracks continued through the long grass to a weathered house set on the edge of the cliffs. A wooden sign read PRIVATE ROAD. The house looked empty, so she skirted the sign and walked around the edge of the field to the rocky shore.

A metal sign, courtesy of Tancook Island Public Safety, warned the rocks were dangerous. A broken cable stretched below the sign. Mottled rock rose up to scrub pines on the ridge. The tide was going out. She climbed onto the first step of rocks, walked towards the island's tip, then pulled herself onto a higher outcrop. The whitened sky was opaque: a day that wouldn't go dark but wouldn't get sunny. Damp wind ruffled her hair, and she clapped the grit off her palms. In the wind, she sometimes heard something faraway, like voices behind a closed door. She tried not to worry about them. They were like a migraine; if she feared them too much, she might bring them on. But the faint sibilance was like a conversation she could only hear a part of. She wanted to know what the voices would tell her. After all, they were part of her, and they might tell her some true thing about herself, something she couldn't get at any other way.

A faint path ran along the ridge then merged with an old logging road heading into the forest. The intermittent cries of birds rose and settled. The remnant of road led into a forest of slender poplars and elms, and then dwindled to no more than a deer trail. Finally, the forest opened onto a clearing, the far side hemmed by the edge of a pine forest, but there was something strange about the black-green trees. Walking closer, Francoise saw the trees were loaded with feathery, pale green moss hanging like heavy nets of tangled hair. The moss dangled over the pine branches in clumps like pale green snow, a scene from a fantastic picture book. She touched the moss, tough and wiry against her fingers. She must come back and paint this.

A crooked fire circle set under the pine trees, a crinkled wrapper, a faded beer can—kids must come here. She walked deeper in. The forest ended just before the edge of cliffs that dropped down to a broad rocky shelf, and down again to black boulders resting like dark animals in the water.

She sat next to the edge and looked out over the boulders and the ocean. Had her uncle ever come here? She tried to conjure some picture of him, and then, distinct and clear as a bird, the second voice spoke.

He's coming.

Its clarity was undeniable; it felt strange to hear it outdoors. She didn't move. It unnerved her to hear the voice without any sense of directionality.

"My uncle?"

No. This voice was the patient one. Francoise felt a sense of expectation; there was something she was supposed to understand.

"My father?" As she spoke, she understood: everything made sense. Her uncle must have known, all along, where her father was. This place was for them to see each other. It was perfect. She felt a thrumming energy, an almost unbearable excitement. And then the third voice. Its presence urged caution; it seeped, large and dark, below the other voices.

"I know," she whispered. "He'll be nervous about seeing me. It will probably be a little strange at first."

She picked herself up off the grass. She imagined the full ashtrays at the house, the breakfast dishes left unwashed. She had to go and get ready. She hurried back, past the forest with its pale, heavy moss, past the clearing and into the trees. She would bring her father here. She would show this to him. She ran down the trail toward her uncle's house.

When she got inside, breathing hard, thick silence absorbed her. She had doubted the voices, but maybe this was what they'd been for all along.

Francoise moved to the kitchen to begin washing up. She would take the ferry to Chester and get more groceries so she could make a nice dinner. She swirled soap onto a dish and wondered if she should go down to the pier for the next ferry's arrival.

In the bedroom she brushed out her hair. Her cheeks were red. Her hair floated from the brush. And then she heard the high wispy giggle, the first voice, amused at her excitement. It didn't say anything, but she heard its small laughter in the corner. She clenched her hairbrush.

It'll be fun. The voice giggled like a girl at a slumber party.

"Shut up," Francoise said. "I don't need you now." Shaking, she bent over and brushed from the nape of her neck.

I'll bet he's very handsome. The voice came from the corner, teasing her.

"Shut up!" Francoise shouted. She straightened and stared at herself in the mirror. The mark on her cheek accentuated her eyes. "You have to be quiet when he comes," she said. She pushed her hair back. She would go now and meet him. She would watch from the road for the ferry's approach, watch for the small darkness on the horizon to come to her and take its shape.

Spillover

Boston had been my home since college, and I always vowed I'd never move back to Manhattan. I didn't want to live on the same island as my mother and Husband Number Three. As far as I was concerned, Ron had married her for her rent-controlled apartment. My mother wasn't overbearing, just the opposite. She floated through life in soft focus, a real Valium queen. I came out to her when I was in high school, but she clung to the idea that my being a lesbian was a phase or a rebellion. The fact that Kaiya was black added weight to her theory. The one time they met, my mother could barely land on earth. It was spring, and all she could talk about was hats, as if her meager concentration was focused on the small space of air above our heads.

KAIYA GOT UP from the table, rolling up a shirt cuff where she had lost a button. Her house clothes, unraveling at the shoulders and elbows, seemed thin and temporary against her body; the intimacy of these small imperfections pleased me. I'd bought her a silk kimono to mark our first anniversary, and I planned to give it to her that night. She'd recently been offered a job as a reference librarian at Cooper Union in New York, and mostly, we had avoided talking about it.

"Let's go to the Gardner Museum this afternoon," I said.

Kaiya leaned into the refrigerator, humming a little tune. "Pineapple and ham omelets?" she proposed. I made a face. Kaiya was born in St. Lucia, but she'd gone to school in England where she learned to like big English breakfasts. She made her own tropical variations. Clutching a fork in her fist, she'd grin and imitate a television commercial, exclaiming how something was healthy and good-tasting too. I laughed at the unnatural way her mouth moved when she imitated an American twang. Schooling had softened her island accent, encased it in proper diction, but in moments of excitement or anger her voice slipped into the lilt of water and sun.

She stood up, "It's such a nice day. It's not so hot. Let's do something outside."

I studied her feet: the slight pink of her toenails, the silver bracelet on her ankle.

"I don't want to go without you," she said.

I rose and put my face on her shoulder, whispering into her neck. "I'll go," I said. "We'll go."

I DIDN'T TELL MY MOTHER I was moving back. Once upon a time, I had my mother's dark blonde hair, but over the years, I'd dyed mine purple, black, and spiky-white. My mother always had a matching purse and shoes; she wore eyeshadow that complemented her clothes. I pierced my nose; I never wore makeup; I carried a backpack. The resemblance between us was unmistakable.

THROUGH A FRIEND, Kaiya heard about a one-bedroom sublet in Soho, and the next weekend, we took the train to Manhattan to check it out. When we stepped out of the subway at Bleecker Street, I took her hand. I still had that proud, almost-disbelieving feeling when I walked down the street with her. She was tall, dark-skinned, her beauty was in the way she carried herself: dignified but relaxed, her wide shoulders open. Kaiya rarely hurried. She had a way of figuring things in her head, and by the time she took action, her movements seemed almost orchestrated. Making love was the only time her languor broke over into wanting or impatience. Sometimes, watching her in a room full of people, I thought of those moments when she was greedy for my hands and mouth, and I felt a satisfaction in being able to bring her to that, in knowing this side of her that others didn't see.

But apart from those moments, something in Kaiya was beyond me. Maybe that was why I wanted her so much, and why, in bed, I teased her to the point of pleading. For me, it was a game: it brought her pleasure and had a definite conclusion. But Kaiya's withholding was not a game; her separateness was like an unfamiliar taste, a hint of something that can't be named. When she spoke to her mother on the phone, her voice rose and fell in cadences that reminded me how much of her life was outside the boundaries of our life together. I tried to picture her growing up on an island, or as an awkward young woman in a school uniform, but these images were hard to connect with the knowing woman who smiled at me lazily as we walked down Bleecker Street.

We turned on Thompson Street, passed a Tibetan restaurant, a sushi bar, a boutique clothing store. We found the building and buzzed to be let in. The lobby was small and dark, dark enough to hide the dirt, as Kaiya described it later. On the third floor, a woman wearing braces, the clear plastic kind that are supposed to be less noticeable, opened the door. We made polite introductions as we sized each other up.

"Oh, hi." She stepped back to allow us in. "It's small, so you don't exactly need me to give you a tour." We walked into the single room that served as the living space and kitchen. The woman kept brushing her bangs out of her eyes, and it was hard to tell if she was nervous or had some kind of tic.

"I'll let you look around and see what you think. I want to go across the hall for a minute."

The only windows opened onto an airshaft, and a hazy block of light stretched across an exposed brick wall. Chinese statues rested on low bookshelves crammed with books. In the bedroom, a double bed covered with an Indian tapestry almost filled the room; another tapestry billowed from the ceiling.

"Where's the lava lamp?" Kaiya giggled.

It was as if the bedroom and the living space belonged to different people. We sat on the bed, and I bounced on it, testing it.

"What do you think?"

"It's perfect." Kaiya lay back on the bed and stared up at the patterned cloth. "I am so happy to get this job, but I can't imagine coming here alone." She ran her index finger down my arm and took my hand. "I think we could be happy here."

The slope of her cheeks, her rounded nose, made an elegant silhouette in the shadowed room. I leaned over and kissed the soft place above her collarbone.

"We should lock the door," I whispered.

"—and make lots of noise." Kaiya laughed.

The woman returned; she knocked on the door jamb and waited outside the doorway.

"It's great," I said. "We'll take it."

She was very particular about the logistics of our sublet: we would pay her and she would pay the landlord. We shouldn't volunteer information to anyone. Her instructions should have made me wonder, but illegal sublets were commonplace, and I was happy to find an apartment close to Kaiya's job, in a neighborhood removed from my mother's. The arrangement didn't strike me as suspicious at the time.

I DIDN'T WANT to tell my mother I was moving back to the city, but that seemed too unkind. My father died of a heart attack shortly after I was born, and when I tried to picture her as a young widow, I could only remember her flirting with lawyers and accountants, my teachers and my doctor. Even as a child, I understood she accomplished things by relying on her beauty. I called a few days after we'd moved in.

"As soon as you get settled, we'll meet for tea at the Plaza."

"Mom, no one who lives here actually does that."

"Well, dinner then. Ron and I will meet you in Midtown."

Midtown. Neutral territory. "I'll check with Kaiya to see what her schedule's like," I said.

KAIYA CAME HOME smiling from her first day at work. "They are so driven! All day they come into the library wanting such precise information for their projects." She dropped her bag on the table and came to sit on the couch beside me. "They know so much and so little. Today, a girl told me that suffering for art is an old-fashioned idea."

Cooper Union had the feel of an art school—lots of students with piercings, tattoos, and black clothes. Her return from work became a late afternoon ritual. I made tea, and she told stories about eccentric student projects. Sometimes we'd start topping each other, making up projects of our own.

"Disposable tea-kettles," she said.

"Contact lenses for the third eye," I countered.

IN BOSTON, I'd managed the Women's Community Bakery, a job my mother referred to as if it were a summer amusement. It didn't take me long to find a job at an organic bakery on St. Mark's Place. The manager, a skinny woman with a purple mohawk, had a serpent tattooed on her right arm and a nose ring with a small skull set on it. She set aside broken cookies for homeless people who came in. I told her where I'd worked, and she looked me up and down.

"You'll start on the first shift. Wednesdays and Sundays off."

I liked the early morning routine, the warm smell of baking, the quiet before customers came in. For as long as I could remember, I'd analyzed problems like a recipe: I weighed the ingredients, their proportions, how certain things combined. As a child, I carried around a copy of *The Baker's Kitchen*, which I studied with showy absorption. But aside from this bratty implication of maternal neglect, I thought of recipes with a certain mathematical pleasure. They allowed for adjustment: you could try again with a little more of this, a little less of that.

EVERY DAY, Kaiya came home with stories about her coworkers, or an anecdote about a student project. One Friday, when I'd been waiting for ages, she called from somewhere in the East Village.

"Sorry I'm late. I stopped to have a beer with some friends." Her voice sounded faraway against music in the background.

"Do you want me to catch a cab and meet you?"

"You can if you want."

I ran my fingers along the exposed brick; suddenly, it felt grubby. "I'll hang here," I said.

When she finally came home, hours later, I focused on my laptop.

"You could have come out to meet us," Kaiya said.

"You didn't sound like you wanted me."

Kaiya blew out of her mouth. "Have it your way then."

I shut the lid of my computer and took a breath. "You didn't sound exactly enthusiastic. And I waited for you, for hours."

"You know, outside of my job, we do almost everything together."

The flatness in her voice terrified me. I put my head down and pressed my palms against my eyes. Blue geometric patterns spun inside my lids.

Kaiya took a long shower while I lay in bed. I punched the pillow then lay still, trying not to think. Suddenly, a screaming rose through the floor. The yelling sounded like an old woman, her furious words unintelligible. Wrapped in a towel, Kaiya ran into the bedroom, and we listened to the garbled shrieking. I couldn't imagine who the woman was yelling at—there was no answering voice. Kaiya climbed into bed and we lay still, whispering to each other, as if she could hear us through the floor. Just as I was about to get out of bed, the screaming stopped. Then it started again, a raging in a language neither of us could understand. I got out of bed, dug around in the tiny closet for a broom, and beat the wooden end against the kitchen floor. The pounding stung my hand. The screaming stopped.

I reached for Kaiya. She took my hand, opened my fingers, then kissed my palm and curled my fingers around the place her lips had been.

"Kaiya—"

"Don't. I don't want to talk tonight."

I put my arms around her and she moved closer to me, and finally we drifted into sleep.

WHEN I WOKE the next morning, Kaiya lay on the far side of the bed. I moved towards her and rubbed my hand over her ribs and down her thigh.

"Kaiya, I'm sorry."

She stretched, then turned to me and opened one eye.

"I overreacted," I said.

"You think? Let's go out, get something to eat, okay?"

We got dressed and walked out into a bright Saturday morning. The Korean guy who owned the corner vegetable stand greeted us as we walked by. Mustached old women in sturdy shoes swept the sidewalks and gossiped with their neighbors. As we crossed Houston Street, a young woman with crimson hair waved at Kaiya.

"She's designing a beehive environment," Kaiya said. "And I've got a new one to tell you."

We sat down and ordered coffee. The buzz of conversation, the multitude of voices and languages, made my jealousy seem, if not less foolish, less important. Kaiya added two heaping teaspoons of sugar to her coffee and leaned back in her chair.

"One student is building a series of webs in a tree—horizontal platforms made of colored nylon rope, like huge hammocks stretched at different levels in the branches." She splayed her fingers wide and held her hands at different heights to show me. "He's doing it somewhere in Prospect Park. He takes the train to Brooklyn every day with piles of nylon rope. Of course, it will only be visible in the early spring and fall, but he wants to invite people to climb up in it, and he wants to photograph it from different angles in each season."

"Someone's going to fall out and he'll get himself sued." I felt old as soon as the words were out of my mouth. "Did he come into the library?"

"Yeah, he originally came in looking for information about spiders, something more than a Google search would tell him. Then, someone tried to steal his rope, and he thought about building a tree-like structure indoors somewhere, and then building his webs in that."

"Spider-Man," I laughed.

Kaiya looked out to the street. "Of course, it was impossible. Trying to build something narrow on the bottom and wide on top—it would be a nightmare. When you start to design something shaped like that, you realize how strong a tree really is." Her smile was indulgent, almost maternal.

"Trees have roots. Sculptures don't."

"Of course, a sculpture would never lose its leaves the way a tree would," she said. "I told him the slow unveiling was part of the dynamic."

"Here's to organicism." I raised my coffee cup.

SEVERAL NIGHTS A WEEK, the woman screamed downstairs, and when I imagined what went on beneath our feet, my complaints about my mother seemed trivial. Still, whenever she called, I cringed at her leisurely tone. She asked how I was, her voice full of concern, and it seemed impossible to refuse a simple request for lunch.

I met her at a restaurant on Madison Avenue. The creamy Italian tile and high ceilings gave the impression of airy elegance, but the place sounded like a high school cafeteria. After we were seated, the maitre d' appeared with Ron.

"Oh sweetheart, I'm so glad you could get away," my mother fluttered.

I scowled. If Ron was invited, then Kaiya should be invited.

After we ordered drinks, and smoothed our napkins on our laps, I told them about the screaming downstairs.

"Perhaps it's just someone playing their television too loud," my mother said.

She was like a meringue, creamy white, full of air. I looked at Ron to see if he had a better grip on reality, but he merely nodded sympathetically.

"Kaiya's parents fought when she was a kid. It was one of the reasons they sent her away to school. I think it reminds her of their arguments."

"It has to affect your relationship," Ron said. "The spillover."

It was the first thing he'd said that halfway made sense.

"I have a friend who scouts for apartments," he said. "I'd be happy to take care of her fee for you." He leaned forward in his chair. His shirt and cuffs were spotless.

"It's nice of you to offer, Ron." I reached for a breadstick, broke it in half, and took a bite.

After lunch, my mother touched up her lipstick as the waiter set down her coffee. "Would you like to come up to the apartment?" she asked.

"I have to get back to work," I lied.

Outside, we said our goodbyes. My mother kissed me on the cheek and left a lipstick smudge.

"Don't let Kaiya catch you with that," Ron grinned.

WHENEVER THE SHRIEKING rose through the floor, it started without any warning rattle; then the yelling grew louder, more raucous, building toward a climax that never happened. We'd never seen anyone go in or out, and we imagined the woman was crazy, shouting at memories.

One night, after we'd come home from seeing a movie, the screaming started again, but this time, there was another voice, the sound of someone trying to soothe her.

"She could hurt someone. We should call the police," Kaiya said.

When she picked up the phone, everything around her seemed bright—her sage green coat against the brick wall, the arc of lamplight on her wrist. She gave her name and then paused and put her hand over the receiver.

"They want to know who's making the complaint," she whispered.

"Just say we're neighbors."

"We're neighbors," she stuttered. "We don't want her to come after *us*. That's all I can say." She hung up.

We stood looking at each other. There was an angry yell, then silence.

"Let's go for a walk," Kaiya said. "I can't take this."

ON SUNDAY MORNING, Kaiya took a shower while I read the news. As soon as she emerged, the shrieking started downstairs. I stood up.

"Come on," I said. "I'll take you somewhere quiet."

"Is there anywhere quiet on this blessed island?"

I took her uptown to the Frick Collection. I loved going to museums with her: Kaiya saw things I didn't—the way light fell in a picture, a detail I hadn't noticed. Back in Boston, on our first date, I'd worn a vintage dress, a floppy hat, and pretended I was Isabella Gardner. I led her around the Gardner Museum, telling her where and when I bought certain pieces. We laughed so hard that a guard asked us to be quiet.

At the Frick, we sat for a while in the fountain courtyard. The pale green light soothed me, and I leaned against Kaiya. I wished we could stay peaceful like this, enveloped in soft light.

When we got up to look at the pictures, they were hung in the same order I remembered. We stopped in front of a Vermeer, *Girl Interrupted at her Music.*

"They're having artistic differences," I laughed.

"You always see a conflict," Kaiya said.

"What do you mean?"

"You see a music student disagreeing with her teacher about how something should be played, right?"

"It's just a game," I said.

"All the same."

I RESOLVED TO BE EASIER to live with—less salt and more sugar. The next night I made ravioli stuffed with butternut squash, a light cream sauce—I knew she would love it. I hummed as I rolled out the pasta, dabbed the pureed squash inside the squares, and pressed the edges together. Ron called as I was cooking. His smooth voice was an intrusion, and I got him off the phone as quickly as I could. His attraction was so obvious, and so foolishly couched in paternal concern.

When Kaiya came home, she hung up her coat and set a bottle of wine on the table.

"I'm making something special for dinner."

She smiled wanly and kissed me hello. "It smells wonderful."

She opened the wine and poured two large glasses.

"Ron called a little while ago, supposedly about an apartment."

Kaiya raised one eyebrow.

"I swear, I think he's jerking himself off when he talks to me on the phone. He asks me the most simpleminded questions, then his voice gets kind of different."

"Oh please," Kaiya said. "Not before eating."

"I can't help it. He bothers me."

"What doesn't?"

I imagined myself splitting like a cartoon ghost and stepping out of my own body. My shadow lifted the hot skillet and poured our dinner over the pots in the sink. I turned to the stove. The cream sauce was starting to thicken. I held my breath, stirred, then turned down the flame. When we sat down to eat, I lit a candle for peace.

MY MOTHER CALLED one afternoon to say she had sprained her ankle in Pilates class. She sounded upset, fuzzy about what had happened. Ron was in LA on business, and I offered to come uptown and do some grocery shopping and errands.

My mother still lived in the apartment where I grew up, and it had remained her realm, as if her husbands had only a peripheral effect on her life. She lay on the couch with a novel. The bandage on her ankle, fluffy and white, looked like the bulky bandages worn by racehorses. Happy and flushed, she was like a child who had conned her way into staying home from school. We talked for a few minutes, and I walked around the living room looking at photos of myself: a beautifully framed catalogue of every awkward age. She handed me a list, and asked if I would mind getting her some ibuprofen before I left.

In the bathroom, the blue and white tiles and matching towels were just the same. I remembered standing on a step stool so I'd be tall enough to brush my teeth and spit into the sink. I remembered my mother dampening a comb under the tap, carefully parting my hair, and lifting me up to look in the mirror. I used to lock myself in this bathroom to examine the new hairs growing under my arms, between my legs. The thick hairs against my pale skin horrified me; my mother was perfectly sleek and smooth everywhere.

The medicine cabinet was jammed with Valium in several denominations of milligrams, sleeping pills, muscle relaxers, and various anti-depressants. I reached for a little container of Valium, poured a few pills into my hand, then stood there, shaking them in my palm like dice. The florescent bulb flickered. I dropped them into my shirt pocket and cupped two ibuprofen in my palm.

RIDING DOWN IN THE ELEVATOR, I thought about how nothing seemed to pierce my mother's fog. She hadn't asked about Kaiya. She never did. I took a Valium out of my pocket, set it on the back of my tongue, and swallowed.

I stopped on the corner to read my mother's list, and her neatly tilted handwriting made me pause: Epsom salts, deodorant, dental floss, milk, grapes, bread. Something tingled along the back of my neck; the sounds of the street grew quiet. My mother's elegance had always seemed purchased, and therefore false, but looking at her ordinary requests, I felt my neck and face get hot. Had the medicine cabinet been full of things to ease her when my father was alive? Maybe not. Her second husband divorced her for reasons she never explained. Of course, I'd never asked. I saw myself as a child: pretty but sullen, ignoring my stepfathers, burying myself in the pages of a cookbook. The heat moved down my chest and spread across my stomach. I'd complained about my mother for years, her predictability and shallowness, as if she were a cartoon, but standing on the corner of 79th Street, I felt her colors filled in.

AFTER DOING MY mother's errands, I met Kaiya at Café Orlin for dinner.

"Something happened this afternoon," I began. "I realized something about my mother."

Kaiya stiffened.

"It's not a complaint."

"I didn't know you had any other kind of thing to say." She looked off into the crowd.

I'd felt so good—couldn't she tell I was trying? I chipped at the label on my Dos Equis. We watched the passing crowd and ate our dinner in silence.

When we walked into the lobby of our building, unmuffled shrieking echoed against the tiles. I hurried up the stairs. A toothless old woman with scraggly hair yelled into the doorway of the apartment below ours. A stained housecoat covered her sagging breasts. Loose flesh under her chin shook as she screamed.

"What is wrong with you?" I yelled and pointed upstairs. "We listen to you scream all night."

Seeing me pointing upstairs, she opened her wide, dark mouth and jabbered in an unknown language. She stamped her foot in time with her pumping fist. I understood she was imitating me, pounding a broom on the floor.

"Yes, that's me. What the hell do you mean, yelling at all hours of the night?"

A middle-aged woman, who didn't seem to speak English, peeked out of the apartment. The old woman raised her arms above her head and brought them down slowly, her fingers wiggling. She repeated the motion, over and over. Her soiled clothes, her frantic mouth and whiskered chin, made her look like a demented gnome imitating rain.

"Enough!" I yelled.

The woman scuttled into the apartment, then reappeared, holding a large kitchen knife. The wide blade, flecked with whatever she'd been cutting, shone gray in the dark hall.

"Aaah!" She shrieked and pointed a grubby finger at the ceiling.

Kaiya tugged on my shoulder.

"Police!" I told her. "We're going to call the police."

She waved the knife and pointed it upward. Kaiya grabbed my arm, and we ran up the stairs. I slammed the door and turned the deadbolt.

"She's like something from a horror movie."

"Worse," Kaiya said.

Adrenaline pounded in my head and chest. "If we make a formal complaint to the police or Bellevue, we'll give ourselves away."

Kaiya nodded.

I took a deep breath and tried to think. I didn't want to go out again. The clock read 9:37—it seemed so much later. "Maybe we should take Ron up on his offer to help us find a place."

"I'm going to take a bath," Kaiya said. "And try to calm down."

When Kaiya finally came to bed, damp and warm, I touched her, tentatively.

"I can't," Kaiya said. "Downstairs. It's too much."

I rolled away and turned in the other direction. She moved up behind me and curled herself around me.

"I'm sorry, it's just everything." She kissed my shoulder and slipped her arm around my waist. I lay there for what seemed like hours, concentrating on the motion of her breath against me, the softness of her belly rising and falling against the small of my back.

I TOLD MYSELF that things weren't unraveling, it was just a bad time that was bound to get better. I took something from my mother's medicine cabinet every time I visited. I visited more and more often. One Saturday, I went uptown to do some errands for her, and when I got there, Ron was home. I walked into the kitchen to get something to drink, and he followed.

"It really means a lot to your mother that you've been willing to come uptown and help."

"It's not a big deal, Ron. I get off work early since I go in so early."

"How's Kaiya?"

"She's fine." I shut the refrigerator with my hip. His solicitous tone made me sick.

In the bathroom, I took two Valium and deposited a few more in my shirt pocket. I looked to see what else I might want. Xanax. I took some of those and put them in the front pocket of my jeans.

AT BREAKFAST THE NEXT MORNING, I sat with a cup of coffee, fiddling with a pack of pastels Kaiya had brought home. I drew a bright green line on an envelope.

"We need to look for another apartment."

"It seems like we just moved," Kaiya sighed.

Using Craigslist seemed a bit dubious, so I looked at classifieds in the *Village Voice* and started texting prospects. Since practically no one's phone number was linked to their geographical location anymore, I got a big sheet of paper and used different colored pastels to rate our prospects.

"Can you come look at some of these with me?"

Kaiya sighed. "I can try to meet you after work, but could you look first since you know the neighborhoods?"

I nodded.

ON MY DAY OFF, I set out for a long day of apartment hunting. I'd only bring Kaiya to see the ones that were promising. I spent the morning on the Lower East Side, then worked my way toward a place in the East Village I'd seen advertised on a bookstore bulletin board. It was another sublet, but anything would be better than what we had. The afternoon was bright, and I strolled along the east side of Tompkins Square Park, thinking about what I'd eat for lunch, when I saw Kaiya and a young man sitting outside at a café. She was holding a spoon, her dark arm stretched toward him, offering him a bite to eat. She smiled, urging him to try whatever it was, and her gesture was so intimate that I reached for the fence and held on. A man. In my worst, most painful fantasies, I had not imagined this. I was sometimes afraid she would meet another woman, someone older and wise, someone famous, an artist or a musician maybe. I knew she had been with men before, but a long time ago. Her mouth moved, and I knew she was saying something slyly funny. Sure enough, he laughed.

I turned into the park and sat down on a bench. The muscle of her arm, the line of her shoulder stretched out toward him—I saw it when I closed my eyes. I dug in my pocket for some Valium. Nothing. I put my head between my knees and tried to breathe. I stayed like that until a homeless guy sat down beside me and started muttering. I smacked the bench seat, then walked out of the park, hailed a cab, and gave my mother's address. She'd told me she had a doctor's appointment, but I had a key.

At the building, I hurried past the doorman and let myself in. The lights were out. Quiet. I went to the kitchen for a plastic bag, then went to the bathroom and opened the medicine cabinet.

I wanted to sweep everything off the shelves. I wanted to open each bottle, dump the loose pills into my bag, and leave the bathroom scattered with empty, orange containers, but later on, I wouldn't know which pills were which, so I picked up bottles and read what they were for. I took every bottle that contained something potent. I couldn't believe my mother hadn't said anything about all the Valium I'd taken over the past few weeks. Was she so spaced out she didn't notice? I pressed my palm against the cool, blue tiles. Did my mother suspect Ron of stealing her pills? Was she afraid to say anything to him? To me? I poured some Valium into my palm and stared at them. No amount of pills could stop the quaking inside me. I threw them into the plastic bag, closed the cabinet, and let myself out.

No way was I going back to our apartment to wait for her. I walked across Central Park, over to Columbus Avenue, down to Central Park South. I finally went downtown as it started to get dark. Kaiya was taking off her shoes as I walked in the door.

"I saw you with him. I saw you!"

Kaiya looked up. Her eyes widened, and then her expression became composed.

"What did you see me doing?"

"Eating lunch. Feeding him . . ." I could hardly say it, "like a child—like a lover."

Kaiya folded her beautiful arms. "Well, he is," she said quietly.

"How could you?"

Kaiya started to lace up the sneakers she'd just undone. "I don't think you really want to know." Under the shakiness, her voice had an edge.

"Why him?"

She met my eyes for a moment, then turned away, as if what she was thinking would hurt too much to say.

"I can't believe this. Why did you make me move here, why—"

"Stop it!" she shouted. "I'm sick of this! Do you expect me to pity you? You're always angry, always complaining. You spoil everything that could be nice."

"I can't help how I am!" I tried to think of something reasonable to say, but I felt caught between tears and fury. "I don't see what gives you the right to go out and, and—"

"I have the *right* to do anything I want." Kaiya stood up. "You've been pissed off about one thing or another for months—your mother, Ron—you know what? I don't think there's so much wrong with them. I think it's all in your head." She went into the bathroom and collected her things. "I'm going out," she said. "I won't be back tonight."

When the door closed, I wanted to smash everything in the room, but instead I sat down. I imagined her with him. Him inside her. I felt sick. I sat very still.

THE INTERCOM BUZZED and buzzed. It sounded like an alarm, but I didn't move. Distant voices called my name. Loud knocking battered my door, and finally, I opened it without asking who was there.

"Thank God." My mother hurried in, her coiffed hair oddly out of shape. She hugged me hard.

"What are you doing here?" I felt wooden in her arms.

"What do you think? We've been worried sick. We've been calling you for hours. I went into the bathroom and saw everything gone . . ."

"Kaiya left."

Ron picked up the plastic bag by the door. My mother stared at its contents as if it were completely unfamiliar.

They made me come home with them that night. I tried to argue, but they wouldn't listen. I couldn't remember my mother ever being that insistent.

Kaiya came and took most of her things while I stayed at my mother's for a few days. When I went back to the apartment, I found a letter from Kaiya next to my list of potential apartments. Her letter said a lot of things about anger and jealousy. Seeing the list I'd marked with red and lavender pastel, I put my head down on the table and wept. When I got up to wash my face, small red marks, like lipstick kisses, smudged my forehead and cheeks.

THE OLD WOMAN downstairs still screamed at odd hours, but finally, she made herself clear. One chilly morning I was taking a shower, soaking in the heat and warmth for a long time. I had just gotten out, and wrapped a towel around myself, when there was a pounding on the apartment door; it jumped against its hinges. A sloshing sound lapped outside the door, and then a large, flowing puddle flowed from the bottom of my doorway. Out in the hall, the old woman's gibberish sounded angry and righteous, and I remembered that night on the landing, how she waved her arms up and down, her fingers wiggling. Then I understood. A leak in the pipes. We ran the water, and it leaked in her apartment. I thought of her fury, how pure and undiluted it had been. The dirty water spread out over the floor, and I pictured her waving her arms above her head. I remembered Kaiya behind me, gently tugging on my arm.

And Not to Have Is the Beginning of Desire

Every fall Eleanor watches the new graduate students arrive. They hurry over the freshly waxed floors with no thought of the summer quiet their chattering presence has destroyed. The doctoral students she privately lays bets on: some will finish; some will drop out or have nervous breakdowns; some will become so peculiar they can't function. The poets and fiction writers are the most friendly and quickly develop their own hierarchy—the anointed, the hopeful, the thrilled-to-have-gotten-in. Otto and Katherine, famously married poets, were hired to attract talented students, and now students arrive from all over the country with their laptops and tablets, sleek receptacles of their aesthetic connection to the larger world.

Eleanor is in charge of giving them desks and juggling their teaching assignments. Sometimes she pairs new students with older students; sometimes she puts all the newbies together. She never pairs two African American students because that seems isolating, although she sometimes puts two lesbians together, or two women who might be, not figuring they will become a couple, but that they will take comfort in each other's presence. She never pairs two attractive straight people of the opposite sex. They have enough proximity, fuck like rabbits as far as she can tell, and she doesn't want anyone weeping in her office about not wanting to share a desk with so and so anymore.

Every year the hopeful wave comes in, shining and eager, but by the following year, especially among the poets, the tide turns. Over the past few years, the pattern has become clear, and she's afraid that the cycle of favorites and discards will erupt in violence: amongst the poets themselves, toward Otto and Katherine, she can't say for sure. If she tried to explain it to an outsider, it would seem petty—crabs in a barrel, climbing over one another for recognition—but even the least talented students write their guts out, and the way that Otto and Katherine play them off against each other becomes more precise and cruel each year. Every spring, as sure the wax fades from the floors, the gloss comes off the poets and their happiness, and something dark and hurtful sets in.

I CAN ONLY TELL YOU part of this story. I can tell you the hidden part, the part between us, the part everyone wanted to know. *Did we sleep together? Did she let me....* I stood outside her usual sphere. I was not a poet, not a writer, not a man. When I try to arrive at some version of the truth, I have two perspectives, both limited. I can see all of them: Otto and Katherine, their circle of students, as if looking through a telescope the wrong way, and from that distanced viewpoint, the glamour and mystery and excitement of the group is dissipated by their smallness. Then, as if the telescope were turned around, I can see Marina, the claret curve of her lip, her slender neck, the way she smiles at someone outside the circle of magnified light.

FRANCOISE POURS A GLASS of wine and sets it down on her copy of Bataille's *Eroticism, Death and Sexuality*. Otto told her he would look at the proposal for her dissertation one last time. In the last proposal she submitted, Otto, in his impeccable French, picked apart a phrase in Dalwood's translation, a phrase that Francoise had used to underpin her argument, and he then proceeded to undermine her entire thesis. She lifts the glass to her mouth. Every time she goes to his office, standing outside his closed door, she feels a frisson of expectation, although now she can hardly remember what is imagined and what was real.

She stood in front of his bookcase, a wall of books stretching to the ceiling. Even the titles seemed sexy, portentous, although he discussed them with the distanced air of one for whom everything was theoretical. He searched for a book she must read. Barthes, *A Lover's Discourse.* He stood to reach it on the shelf. Touching the rows of slender spines, she rose to meet him. She stood in a light summer dress, legs slightly apart, a challenge; he reached down and, ever so slowly, slid a finger up the inside of her thigh. The lightness of it, the anticipation, made her wet. "Kneel," he said softly. And she knelt.

I'M AN ORPHAN. Melodramatic, perhaps, but my whole life is inscribed by a loss that has already occurred.

I was adopted as an infant by a high school social studies teacher and his wife. Imagine neatly mowed lawns, laundry airing in the sun, a metal swing set. The family photos, bourgeois and domestic, make it seem as if I belong, but it's all atmosphere and inference. I was a skinny girl with dirt-stained knees, deeply tanned from spending hours poking at anthills, unfeminine from the start. To my adoptive family's credit, they never tried to make me into anything I was not. When I started playing basketball, my father encouraged me to go out for the team. In high school, I developed a consuming crush on a local tennis player. My mother listened to my swooning admiration for months, then signed me up for tennis lessons at the local swim and tennis club.

I want to say that Marina was my guide to the world of poetry and literature, but I grew up with books, filled with the knowledge of a world below everyday surfaces, a world that language made real. Long stretches of my adolescence were spent huddled over a novel, and whenever I started a new book, I had the feeling I was venturing not into *a* world, but into *the* world—a place of complexity and richness below the shopping mall life that surrounded me.

I was finishing a doctorate in Archeology when I met Marina. I had always been the seducer, and then I was seduced. Early on, she loaned me a translation of Barthes' *A Lover's Discourse*. I took this as a sign; I should have seen it was a warning.

TAUT SKIN, FRESH VOICES. Francoise can't stand one more year of watching the bright young things, can't stand watching the way they bloom under Otto and Katherine's attention. If she tried to tell them that everything was not as it seemed, they wouldn't believe her. They would think, *she's mediocre*, or *she's jealous*, or *she's old*. It would be pathetic to explain that she had once been the object of desire. She has been here too long. Otto keeps her endlessly revising the proposal for her dissertation. He explains, in the most reasonable tone, that clearly defining her ideas will save her time and energy, but she has turned in eleven drafts of her proposal, and each time he finds some subtle point to criticize, then collapses her whole castle of cards. She takes a sip of wine and opens her desk drawer to look at the pistol. It's a lady's piece with pearl inlay on the handle, a slender barrel, late nineteenth century. The antiques dealer assured her it would still work.

OTTO AND KATHERINE WALK into the English office together—cheeks flushed, coats open, satchels over their shoulders—like adventurers from afar. They conduct themselves with a willed youthfulness, although Katherine has cut her hair in a middle-aged bob, and Otto's dark hair is thinning.

"Hi, Eleanor." Katherine smiles as if something amusing has just happened. As she and Otto stand at the mailboxes, gathering their mail, Otto leans into her to say something *sotto voce*. Katherine laughs.

Otto turns, as if remembering they're in the presence of others. "Eleanor, if I give you something to scan, could you take care of it this morning?"

"Sure, Otto. No problem." Eleanor understands the masquerade, although it still feels awkward. His voice, warm and courteous, is a mask for his polite withdrawal. When she first arrived, he had asked why she was working as a secretary, as if it were clear that this work was too pedestrian for her abilities. Noticing her interest in Shakespeare, he had praised her intelligence and taste. He left her little notes. Privately, he called her Portia. He never touched her.

The first time he called from his office upstairs, Eleanor was surprised, imagining he wanted some administrative task dispatched. Instead, he said, "Let me read you something," and he read a quote from Wallace Stevens, one she didn't completely understand.

Sometimes he called to ask her advice about something he could have easily decided for himself. When the office was empty, she would tell him a funny anecdote from her day, and his voice, full of intelligence and humor, encouraged her, as if she were fleshing out an idea that had previously been abstract to him. One afternoon, they'd been laughing on the phone, now she can't remember at what, and Katherine had walked into the English office. Hearing Eleanor's laughter, Katherine stiffened.

"Don't imagine I don't know what's going on," Katherine hissed. The lines around her mouth, deepened by anger, made her face an angry mask. Grabbing a sheaf of papers from her mailbox, she hurried out of the office.

FRANCOISE OPENS HER PURSE, puts the pistol inside, and snaps the clasp. She's meeting Otto at noon and wants to know at least one thing he doesn't. He's always a step ahead. Like Orpheus, he turns to see her and sends her back to the shadowy dark. He's had the latest draft of her proposal for a week; all he has to do is approve it so she can begin writing her dissertation.

Walking toward campus, Francoise picks her way around the puddles. The smell of exhaust, wet branches and coffee, waft through the air. Her red cowboy boots make her feel younger, a little saucy, although the feeling fades when she sees Marina coming out of a café near the university. She's accompanied by a woman, a grad student from another department, and rumors have floated through the overheated air of the graduate program. The woman's long face and high forehead give the impression of intelligence, as if she is not to be denied. She wears motorcycle boots, jeans, a scuffed leather jacket; her brown hair falls to her shoulders. Marina stops so the woman can light a cigarette, and she half-turns, shielding the flame from the wind. Francoise can see how it will end—the intense brown-haired woman, her cheeks pocked with acne scars, holding her cigarette like a man— she'll end up with her heart in a blender. Marina smiles at something the woman says and reaches into her coat pocket, like a child fishing for a treat.

ORPHAN, ORFÉE, ORPHEUS. I want to be Orpheus, but I have no song. The first time I saw Marina, I should have guessed she was a poet: sitting in a café with a clutch of laughing grad students. Laughing instead of baring their teeth. I didn't fully understand the competitiveness of poets. I've always loved Rilke, who seems tipped toward the angelic, that tall tree in the ear filtering nascent voices. Rilke, so inept finally, in earthly matters: marrying Clara, communing with Paula and the angels in his requiem.

How to describe Marina? Lovely, Mediterranean, with deep olive skin and black hair shining like obsidian, piled loosely on her head, all the more lovely for the way it slipped from its fastenings. She was slender, small-breasted, and it was obvious that she liked men. She treated them fondly, like boys, as if her touch were not charged, as if they must bear the beauty of her presence without responding.

She was charming. It's a word we don't use much anymore. She was beautiful and understood the difficulties her beauty created. She could be self-deprecating, as if to undercut her beauty and set others at ease. Later, I learned that her need to charm came not from assuredness, but from its absence. Chameleon-like, she didn't change her looks, or her hair; it was not a matter of surface. She immersed herself in the intellectual milieu around her in order to absorb it. She succumbed to the most interesting people around her.

FRANCOISE WALKS INTO the Languages and Literature building, deposits her books on her desk and goes to the bathroom to smooth out her hair, which the dampness makes wild, Medusa-like. Her eyeliner has smeared; the soft skin beneath her eyes is puffy with fine lines. She reaches into her purse for a Q-tip and runs it under her eyes. On her cheek, a birthmark that was once pale brown, distinct, has softened to a smudge. She pulls back her hair and smooths her skirt. The short skirt with cowboy boots is a nice touch. She'll be okay.

Climbing the stairs to Otto's office, her legs feel wobbly. His door is half-open and, hearing his voice on the phone, she knocks softly. He beckons her in, gesturing that she should sit in the armchair.

Her proposal is set in the middle of his neatly arranged desk.

"Yes, yes, I understand." Otto's voice, calm and deep, sounds weary. He looks over at Francoise and rolls his eyes, indicating that the person on the other end is boring him terribly. She feels a flush of hope.

"Yes, J—it's important," Otto says, "and we'll discuss it further, but I have someone here now, so I must go." He uses the poet's first name, so Francoise will know that this is a famous poet who teaches at Iowa, that even the sought-after seek him out. He smiles at Francoise, who smiles back, in spite of herself.

Otto hangs up. "I'm sorry. She does go on, and her concerns always become metaphysical." He smiles, conspiratorial, as if to suggest that the poet has become tedious, that Francoise herself wouldn't fall prey to such clichés in thinking.

She fishes in her purse for a pen and touches the handle of her pistol; its smoothness excites her.

Otto picks up her proposal. "This is better. Your thinking is becoming more clear. But here, on page five," and he flips through the pages. "If you're going to talk about the modern elegy, you need to figure in Ramazani—have you read him?"

"I've heard you're reading him in workshop."

Otto nods, dodging the reference to the class she's not allowed to take this term. "He's excellent on the ways in which the tonality of the modern elegy is different from what came before it. Plath and Lowell, well, he has many different examples, but they don't idealize the dead. There's more anger, more overt hostility, and it's conveyed in their diction."

Otto stands up and moves toward her, as if he might be reaching for her, but he's reaching for a book on the shelf, right behind her shoulder. As he leans over, the smell of his soap mixes with the scent of leather from an old coat. He slides the book out from near her ear, like an uncle doing a magic trick.

"Your section on Cixious is fine, but remember that your own critical stance has to be consistent." Otto makes a note on a piece of paper, as if this is all a simple matter, as if it won't be weeks of work in yet another direction. "Jahan

Ramazani's *The Poetry of Mourning.* If you're going to talk about the elegy in the latter part of the twentieth century, you really must read it."

FRANCOISE WALKS DOWNSTAIRS, fighting back tears. This proposal isn't even required by the graduate school, but Otto claims it is necessary, and now he's sent her back again, like a board game where her piece gets knocked back to the beginning.

At the foot of the stairs, the Director of Composition, a reedy man partial to argyle vests, greets her without seeming to notice her expression.

"Francoise, I was looking for you. Do you have a few minutes?"

She follows him down the hall. Rumor has it he's moved from one research institution to the next, a step up each time, a poster boy for academic success. Inside his office, he turns a palm upwards, indicating the chair opposite his desk. Once she's seated, he puts his fingertips together, like a steeple, in front of his nose.

"Francoise, I'm sorry to tell you that we won't be giving you a teaching assistantship next year. If it were up to me, I'd give you another year and simply say that your dissertation must be done by then, but the new chair has implemented this policy. You've been here for eight years, including the Masters, and it's a university mandate—after six years in a PhD Humanities program, a candidate won't be given additional aid."

She turns to look out the window and tries to take a deep breath, but the view is blurry with tears. She starts to cry silently. Tears seep into her palm. "I'll have visa problems if I'm not enrolled in school. I'll have to go back to Canada, but I've been here for years now. I don't have any family there, I've nothing to go back to."

Cautiously, as if she were an unpredictable animal, he comes out from behind his desk and hands her a tissue. She knows he will be entirely politically correct; he cannot touch her, but she longs for him to place a hand on her shoulder or make some small gesture of comfort.

"I'm sorry," she says. "He won't let me finish. He won't approve the proposal for my dissertation."

"How long have you been working on the proposal?"

"More than a year."

He looks surprised and starts to say something, then stops. "Who else is on your committee? Is there someone else who can direct? Someone who might be more in line with your thinking?"

"Katherine won't do it—she won't go against Otto. And if I'm going to write on twentieth century poetry, and he's not on my committee, how will it look?"

He looks at the wall above her head, as if trying to conjure a diplomatic answer. "I do see the problem," he says.

Francoise stares at the toes of her boots. She turned forty-three a week ago. She will never finish her PhD, never get a real job, never publish a book, never have the approval of the one person who matters most. This morning her boots made her happy, and now they are just pathetic.

IT WAS MARINA'S IDEA to make impressions of our torsos. She'd gotten a tall roll of brown paper and black water-based paint. Along with me, there were four other women at her apartment: two art students, Marina, and another poet. Marina pulled her shirt off over her head, and stood in the middle of the room, naked from the waist up, slender-hipped, considering the thick black paint. She shivered, her brown nipples growing erect.

"Someone will have to paint it on me," she said.

I reached for my glass of wine.

"Who's going to do me?" She smiled, reaching for a paint-brush the size of a ruler. She handed it to me. Trembling, I dipped the tip in the paint then stepped toward her. I touched the delicate skin below her collarbone. She shivered.

"It's cold," she laughed. "I should have let it sit out longer."

Wet, shaking, I wanted her to myself. I was furious the others were there. I would linger on her breasts, make her feel what I felt. I dipped the brush in the paint and reached toward her again.

Later, I would dream it over and over: Marina painting me, the cold black paint covering my breasts, lingering at my nipples. I woke each time, aching between my legs, an aching that felt as if it would never be appeased.

ELEANOR HEARS ABOUT the painting party later. The gossip filters down through the poets and fiction writers as every-one tries to imagine it: five women covering each other in paint, rolling their impressions onto paper on the floor. How artistic.

When Otto comes in on Wednesday morning, the lav-ender circles under his eyes are darker.

He takes papers from his mailbox, checks them carefully, then tucks them under his arm.

"Hello, Eleanor, how are you?"

"I'm fine, Otto." It's as if she's running lines for a play, their words spoken with only a semblance of emotion. She hands him his messages and reminds him of a few depart-mental details.

When Katherine comes in, she's wearing a long skirt with a slit in the side, and through the slit, Eleanor glimpses pale, goose-bumped flesh above the knee. Knee socks. Katherine isn't usually so inept.

"Eleanor, you haven't heard from Marina, have you?"

"No. Why do you ask?"

"We were supposed to have lunch today, but she left a note here." Katherine studies a small note from her mailbox, as if trying to decode a message that isn't there.

"As far as I know, she's been showing up to teach her classes. I haven't had any complaints," Eleanor says.

FRANCOISE OPENS THE FREEZER and takes out a bottle of Absolut. She pours herself an inch or two in a tumbler, sets the bottle on the counter, and wanders into the living room.

She sips the cold vodka—such purity, such power in clear fluid. It always does what it's supposed to do. She had believed she would finish, get a job, move away, but now it's clear that it won't happen. The job market is impossible. Even the bright young things get jobs with heavy teaching loads: four classes a semester, or jobs at community colleges. She will never even have that.

She glances at an old note from Otto, the familiar handwriting that has annotated so many of her poems. When she was younger, she wanted to be a painter, but painting was too abstract; it didn't render what she truly wanted to say, and so she turned to poetry. Otto told her that her vision was rare; he encouraged her—and then he withdrew. She still doesn't know if this is because he decided he'd misjudged, that she really isn't talented, or if he considers her capable, like a parent letting go of a bicycle so she will know she can ride by herself.

Ramazani, *The Poetry of Mourning.* They're discussing it in Otto's workshop, a class she's banned from now. Last year, oh, she hates to remember, she went to class when she'd been drinking. She didn't mean to. She'd gone out to eat before class, met up with a friend, and they'd ordered wine, and never gotten around to the food. At the break, Otto asked her to leave, and the following semester, when she tried to sign up for the graduate poetry workshop, Otto told her that she had taken enough workshops, that she should concentrate on her proposal so she could get to work on her dissertation.

His class meets on Tuesday nights. All week, the graduate students read the assigned poems and essays over their morning coffee, mulling their work as caffeine fans their energy. Each term, Otto chooses a particular theme, bringing together poems and essays from a wide variety of sources, and the brilliance of his seminars is that he's truly widely read, and humble before the art that precedes him. He encourages the students to think of themselves as part of an artistic lineage. His class makes everyone resonate at a higher frequency. Katherine says that, when she teaches the graduate workshop the following semester, she reaps the benefit of Otto's teaching because the students turn in amazing poems in the aftermath of his class. Francoise imagines this is true, but she's been set adrift.

IN THE BEGINNING, I saw Otto and Katherine through the lens of Marina's admiration. I thought of them as fascinating teachers. It wasn't until later that I understood our affair had been an entertainment, a matter of sexual speculation. Marina's absence from their circle, the days she spent with me, provided an erotic study because, together, sipping on their coffees, they knew that I would fail to hold her.

FRANCOISE POURS HERSELF more vodka and adds ice. Everyone will be getting ready for class, the class to which she has been disinvited, the class that the beautiful Marina reigns over.

She sets her tumbler on the floor, grabs her coat and purse, and walks out of the house, leaving the door half-open behind her.

She lives only a few blocks from campus. The slush has frozen in unexpected places, and she starts to slip, but catches herself on a parking meter, the thick nub bumping her breastbone.

The stars blur. It's maybe a half hour before class, the class she can no longer attend. She yanks on the door to the Languages and Literature building. Dark. No one is here yet. She climbs the steps to Otto's office and sees a light under his door. He is preparing for class, communing with the angels. She knocks lightly, then walks in without waiting for a response.

Otto is seated at his desk. His round cheeks are mottled, his expression haggard. Closing the door behind her, she leans against it. The room feels small; the windows tremble. She pulls the pistol from her purse and points it at Otto's heart.

"Francoise, what's happened?" Sweat rises on his forehead, transparent dots like tiny domes. She's never seen him sweat before. "Francoise, please tell me what's wrong." His voice is calculatedly soothing. She hates this. He will say what he needs to in order to calm her.

"I can't do it again! I can't!"

"Francoise, please. It'll be fine." His brown eyes are clear, one slightly smaller than the other. His face is lopsided, as if he's had a stroke. But he hasn't had a stroke.

She is aware of a fresh lucidity: *maybe I can see the future, maybe I know what will happen now.*

"You need to calm yourself," Otto says. "This isn't the way to fix anything."

"It will never be enough! You'll always think of something else." She tries to shout, but her voice is full of holes. She looks at her hand, clenched and shaking, the skin papery and pale. She whispers, épaule. *Shoulder, shoot him in the shoulder.* She begins to cry, feels herself crumpling inside. She doesn't want to shoot him. Doesn't want to hurt him. He is beautiful. He is the best thing that ever happened to her. He helped her see what she could be—but he will never let her have it.

She will change her life, change everything. She turns the pistol to her head, as if in mock salute.

I WANTED TOO MUCH. Marina and I spent three weeks together when spring was on the edge of becoming, but she left me to comfort Otto and Katherine, who were shaken by the suicide of a graduate student, a poet. I'd seen the woman around campus; she dressed in vintage clothes or youthful outfits. She was often by herself, and it was hard to imagine the particular quality of her absence.

We were lying in my bed when Marina's cell phone rang, a foreign chime I didn't recognize. It was Katherine, calling to say that Otto was distraught, people were gathering at the house—would she come? Marina was drawn back into the circle of the anointed, and I was left outside, staring into the light.

ELEANOR HASN'T FELT SORRY for Otto for a long time, but those minutes in his office must have been awful. The chasm of what is possible has opened at their feet. Aside from the police, no one dared ask Otto for details. The university hired someone to clean his office, and his books, a lifetime of reading, were thrown away. Unbearable to have them stained like that.

When she thinks back to her premonition of violence, Eleanor thinks how little she'd really known. She was like a child absorbed in a fantasy—waving a piece of sparkling fabric, whispering to herself—while playing at the edge of a busy freeway.

She had imagined that, when something finally happened, it would expose Otto and Katherine, make everything different, but the students banded together as if Otto and Katherine had been wronged, as if Francoise had done this to them, rather than to herself.

It's rumored that Otto is working on a sonnet sequence of elegies. No one has seen the poems, and Eleanor tries to imagine how the details will be shaped and burnished, whether Otto will cast himself as Orpheus in the retelling of the tale.

She surveys the files on her desk. She has to lay the groundwork for next fall: order desk copies, update the department web page, make desk assignments for the incoming graduate students. Otto presented her with the reading list for next semester's workshop so that she can order books: Robert Calasso's *The Marriage of Cadmus and Harmony*, Rilke's *Sonnets to Orpheus* and *The Duino Elegies*, Helene Cixious, Wallace Stevens.

She gets out the map of desks and list of names. She chooses a pencil, one with a good eraser, and feels an odd, hovering sensation, as if her neck has grown long, her head literally higher. The air hums, buzzing in her ears, and the list of names seems portentous, like doors with something hidden behind them. What are the least combustible combinations? She thinks of commanders choosing regiments to go into battle, how terrible to wield such power. But this isn't the same. She's not responsible. When she sets the pencil's point on the page, the sharp graphite touching the paper, it's as if she's pulling a trigger with a white cloth over her eyes.

III

Catch and Release

The sun warmed Caroline's back, and the smell of earth filled her with something half-forgotten. Green deepened to black at the edges of the coulees. When she first moved to Wisconsin, everyone kept saying this was the driftless region—a place the glaciers hadn't scraped to flatness. In front of them, a wide stream riffled through a pasture. Why had she come with him today? After years of pretending their marriage was fine—that it was just her sister's illness—the excuses about papers to grade or lectures to prepare seemed useless.

"Remember when we used to come here?" Tim flicked his bamboo rod.

She half-covered her eyes against the glare.

"Do you even *want* to be happy?" He drew his arm back and sent his line looping toward the stream.

She pressed her hands into the prickly grass. She had married him after passing her doctoral exams; she'd imagined a marriage of opposites could work. He had caught her with nothing more than kindness and decency, but her youthful gulp seemed foolish now.

He reeled in his line then reached into his vest for a barbless hook. When he looked up towards the bluffs, his profile looked stark, almost noble. Tim saw things she didn't—bird habitats, bat habitats—what he studied was still a mystery to her. The bluffs above the Mississippi were a natural habitat for bats, but they also found their way into people's homes and nested in their attics. Tim had turned his boyhood preoccupations into a grown-up job. He had worked with an older man, long since retired, and they built a business together. Wisconsin Bat Specialists. They climbed up under the eaves and installed mesh doors that let bats out, but wouldn't let them back in. Exclusion. Tim wouldn't call it Pest Control. Now, he had so much business that he'd hired an assistant, and he made more money than Caroline did as a professor. People called him, day and night, especially women. *Please come*, they said. *Please. It's worth anything to me.*

Lovejoy

Caroline had been sleeping with Richard for most of the school year and was thinking about the best way to break it off, when he called her at home, early one morning. The unexpected ringing startled her into fear.

"It's Mickey, he fell off the bluffs." Richard's voice was hoarse. "I have to meet my wife at the hospital. Would you have Elsa cancel my classes?"

"Of course," Caroline said. "Go on. I'll talk to you later." She hung up the phone and pulled her robe around her. The bluffs, visible from her kitchen window, rose against the sky. On overcast days, they reminded her of a scene in a Chinese scroll—steep mountains shrouded in mist. On clear days, they glowed copper and umber, tinting the river town below.

She put water on to boil, then sat down at her kitchen table. He had stumbled and said 'my wife.' He was usually careful to say: 'my children's mother,' a way of declaring his singleness. She had never met Emily, but whenever Richard mentioned some disagreement, usually involving the children or finances, Caroline thought he never seemed to realize, in his brief reporting, how much they were alike.

On their second date, Richard told her that his marriage had ended by the time his children were teenagers. As he looked at her across the table, turning his fork in his hand, Caroline wondered if she detected a practiced sincerity. From other sources–small town gossip really–she knew that he had left his wife for someone younger, so Richard's negligence, in her mind, was that he failed to report his midlife crisis as such. He could be selfish like that, and his selfishness was one reason she allowed herself to start sleeping with him. She'd never have to feel responsible for him in the way she had once felt responsible for her husband, who she had married long ago in a burst of optimism. They had little in common and finally divorced; she tried to think of her marriage as a healthy mistake. Richard was a different matter: well-traveled, a witty conversationalist, unselfish in bed, but she suspected this last attribute was partly a matter of pride, and partly because the benefit of his generosity came back to him so directly.

She waited until after eight o'clock to call his secretary in the History Department. Caroline told Elsa that she wasn't sure whether the boy was alive, although she gathered from Richard's tone that he had been very badly hurt. She asked Elsa to notify the Dean of Students. Mickey was a sophomore at the University.

When she got off the phone, Caroline sat down at the table and pressed her palms against a mug of tea. She would be required to act the part of the helpful companion. She didn't mind, she owed Richard that, but she couldn't provide any real relief. His children had not forgiven him. Mickey was an unhappy boy. "A bit like Eeyore," Richard once said. She had never met his daughter, a senior at Madison.

Caroline and Richard's involvement had been easily navigable in terms of their colleagues, although Caroline found it irksome that once people realized you were sleeping with someone, they wanted to make you a serious couple. It was a polite, Midwestern thing to assume. They both taught at the University of Wisconsin-La Crosse. She was in Economics; he chaired the History Department. They were sometimes invited to the same functions, and those who knew about them accepted them without fuss, but Richard was starting to rely on her for little things, wifely duties, and she didn't want that. She was going to England on sabbatical next year and planned to leave in the summer. A few months ago, when Richard suggested he might come visit, she politely deflected his suggestion. She thought that if she broke up with him at the end of the semester, she would avoid prying questions from colleagues, and it would be a year, or more, before she saw him again.

She expected to hear from him that night, and when she didn't, she imagined that Mickey had died, or was close to it, and Richard was at his bedside. At dinner time, she made herself some toast; she didn't want to linger in the kitchen where the glow of sunset lit the bluffs.

AT THE WAKE, Richard introduced Caroline as his 'friend.' Under a sleek cap of brown hair, Emily had the blanched look of a person in shock. Her brown eyes were huge and fish-like in her narrow face. Caroline recognized the expression: moving forward without a compass. She had felt that way through the long vagaries of her sister's illness, even more when the doctor tried to explain why her sister had died.

"I'm so sorry," Caroline said. "If there's anything I can do, please let me know."

Emily looked confused, and Caroline remembered this feeling; how a veil of grief was like a scrim between her and everything she saw.

"I lost my sister, very suddenly, a few years ago," Caroline said. She felt awkward as soon as she said it. "Of course, it's not the same thing, but…" She couldn't finish. She was making it worse.

Emily's chin trembled; she pressed her lips together. A young woman came up behind her, put her suntanned arms around Emily's waist, and rested her chin on Emily's shoulder.

"This is our daughter, Natalie," Emily said. "This is Caroline, a friend of your father's."

The girl straightened up and looked at her, appraising.

Natalie had a face that should be painted: round and smooth, with a watchful expression, hazel eyes flecked with gold. She looked as if she came from Zagreb or Trieste, as if she were a Romani girl, a changeling, and couldn't truly have been born to Emily and Richard with their narrow, quizzical faces. She wore a long black skirt, a black vest, but her shirt, the color of a new leaf, was pale and translucent against her skin. A macramé choker with a small clay bead rested at the base of her throat. The string had a patina of sweat and dirt on the top.

Natalie gazed at her, and Caroline had an odd sensation of being seen through, as if it were clear that she wanted to leave Richard, but it would be awkward to do so now, as if Natalie understood her pretense. Caroline had a sudden image of pushing Natalie's choker aside, kissing her dirty neck.

Caroline murmured a greeting. She scarcely knew what she said.

"Nice to meet you," Natalie said.

A small group had arrived, and the murmur of muted greetings shifted by the doorway. Caroline, grateful for the diversion, stepped back to let them speak to Richard and Emily.

On the other side of the room, Mickey's friends huddled together, their hands in their pockets, their hair gelled or wet, as if they'd been shoved into a shower and then forced to appear in public. They looked like recalcitrant calves, herded towards slaughter, and kept their restive distance on the other side of the closed casket.

Caroline moved off to the side, pretending to examine the ugly wallpaper, when Natalie came to stand beside her. She looked across the room at her parents, standing together, talking to someone Caroline didn't know.

"Your father should go back to your mother," Caroline said.

Natalie glanced at her, then folded her arms. "He never should have left."

Caroline nodded.

"Why are you with him if you don't like him?" Natalie asked.

"I didn't say I didn't like him."

"Here's Gina," Natalie said, as if this explained something. Gina moved toward them, looking neither left nor right. She had dark hair, a sullen mouth, and glasses with heavy black frames. Urban artist wear. A spiky tattoo circled her left wrist, and her sturdy calf was covered with an elaborately colored monster from *Where the Wild Things Are*. Gina hugged Natalie long and hard, and they stood together, swaying in grief, in the middle of the room.

AFTER THE WAKE, they all retreated to their separate places, like a boxing ring, Caroline thought, each resting in his or her corner. She flopped on her couch in front of the television and picked up the remote. Since Pamela's illness, there was very little she could stand to watch. No hospital shows, no courtroom dramas, no shows about children who were sick or in pain. She did like the mysteries on public television. While Pamela was sick, Caroline became peculiarly attached to a show called *Lovejoy*. The show was set in a cozy version of England, and the main character was a good-humored, politically incorrect womanizer—a person one didn't have to worry about. She liked his mischievousness, that he broke the rules and got away with it. He had an alcoholic old friend, full of arcane knowledge, who was not a realistic drunk, but an endearing one. Caroline imagined living in a thatched roof cottage, drinking tea and reading books. She wanted to be surrounded by green fields, wanted warmth in the midst of cold, history at the center of the swirling world around her. She wanted to accept the eccentricities of her neighbors with a benign humor. She wanted a life that was the opposite of her life right then: Pamela's illness, the endless and grasping series of tests, the chill of fluorescent lights, bedpans and IVs, the horrific way that illness had taken her sister.

When they were younger, Pamela looked like a figure in a pre-Raphaelite painting: long chestnut hair, elegant, snooty features. She and Caroline looked alike, although Caroline always thought of Pamela as sharper, freshly minted, while she, Caroline, was the slightly blurry copy. When they were girls, Pamela had always been ahead of her, and Caroline remembered the way her sister grew beautiful before her eyes, telling her how boys acted, how they liked to be touched, how it felt when they touched her. Caroline felt as if her knowledge of men had been sieved through Pamela, who relayed her experiences without ever asking if Caroline wanted to hear them. *First, he did this*, Pamela said, running her finger along the inside of Caroline's knee. *Then he touched me, here.* Caroline shivered. Pamela had loved her husband, Bryce, but sometimes, Caroline felt as if Pamela's love had been acted out, partly for her benefit, behind a screen of domesticity. Pamela had forced her to become a voyeur.

Bryce owned a store that sold and installed woodstoves and gas fireplaces. Early on, Pamela had confided her fears that the business would never come to anything. She wanted to stay home with their two little girls, but Bryce's business was slow to take hold, and Pamela continued to teach Special Education classes at the local elementary school; her salary kept them afloat. Finally, Bryce's business had blossomed. He hired extra men. When Pamela was finally diagnosed, he wanted to take her on a trip, let her quit her job, but it was too late.

Caroline juggled her grading and preparation for lectures around taking Pamela to the hospital and the girls to their various activities. Of course, Bryce took time off too, but Caroline's husband was often left to fend for himself.

"Your sister's illness is running our lives right now," he once said.

"My god, she's my *sister*. What do you expect?"

"I'm not saying it's wrong. I don't know what they'd do without you. I'm just saying that we've organized our lives around her treatment, and you should recognize that. You need some time for yourself. Your friend Zoe called the other day and joked that I must not give you your messages."

She didn't think their marriage failed because of Pamela, but they all believed that Caroline stepping in to help was temporary, that the doctors would figure out this auto-immune thing, but Pamela got pneumonia in the fall, and then died from sepsis while they were waiting for her long recuperation to begin.

RICHARD AND EMILY HANDLED Mickey's funeral arrangements, and Caroline tried to be helpful, which mostly meant staying out of the way. She wondered why Richard hadn't said more about Natalie, who he'd mentioned only vaguely. Of all the things that Richard could be obtuse about, failing to mention Natalie's rarity seemed his most glaring oversight.

ON FRIDAY NIGHT, Caroline met her friend Zoe for dinner downtown.

"You should come to London for a few weeks," Caroline said. She picked up a French fry and looked at it dubiously. "Think of it—tea at Harrod's, the British Museum, disgusting pub food. It'll be great."

"The bookstore's so busy in the fall," Zoe said.

"Oh, please. I know you hold the place together, but they could manage for a little, couldn't they?"

"Why me, instead of Richard?"

"You're more fun."

"No, really."

"Yes, really. He's angst-ridden already. Now he's going to be further depressed."

"Stop. He's lovely."

"Have him yourself then," Caroline said.

Zoe laughed.

After dinner, Caroline walked up Pearl Street, past the old-fashioned candy store, the bookstore where Zoe worked, a beauty school where students got their hair cut. A few doors up, a bar called CASINO sported an old-fashioned neon sign: *Lousy Service.* Two young women hurried out the door; one was chasing the other. Gina and Natalie.

"Lug!" Gina shouted. "Fucking lug!" She shoved Natalie, who deflected the hit by spinning to the side. Gina stumbled, then caught herself against the brick wall. Caroline hurried toward them.

"Please, stop! What's going on?"

Gina's glasses were crooked, her eyes streaming. "I can't believe you!" she shouted at Natalie.

Natalie walked toward Caroline as if she was stepping out of the ocean, heading for dry land.

"Do you have a car here?"

"Of course," Caroline said. They hurried away, leaving Gina shouting on the sidewalk, pounding her fist against the brick wall.

They didn't speak until they had turned the corner. Caroline hit the remote, unlocking her car doors. Natalie slid into the passenger side.

"Are you all right?" Caroline asked.

Natalie nodded, her eyes tearing up.

"Why in the world was she calling you a lug?"

Natalie pressed the door lock. "L-U-G. Do you know what it stands for?"

"No."

"Lesbian Until Graduation."

"Oh."

"She gets like this. She's raving."

Caroline started the car. She was perhaps fifteen years older than most of her students and often had these moments of feeling impossibly far away from them. She didn't have the same references. Once, in a lecture on labor economics, she had worked in a few references to the show *Parks and Rec*, and she'd been pleased to see a glint of recognition on the students' faces, but the show was off the air now, ancient history in their terms.

"Where do you want to go?" Caroline asked.

"Well, I was staying with Gina, but it doesn't look like that now."

"Do you want to me to drive you to your mother's?"

"If you don't mind, that would be great."

Caroline turned north, toward Onalaska, and Natalie directed her through the suburban neighborhoods. From Richard, Caroline knew that Emily still lived in the house they had shared. As they drove through the quiet streets, Caroline asked. "Have you and Gina been together a long time?"

"We're not really a couple," Natalie said. "We were a while ago, but she still feels... proprietary, I guess."

Caroline pulled up in front of a split-level house on a cul-de-sac. It was hard to distinguish one house from another in the dark, and she wondered if part of Richard's leaving had been precisely that—a flight from the ordinariness of it all.

SINCE THE MORNING of Mickey's death, her private conversations with Richard had been hurried and mostly taken up with logistics. When she encouraged him to spend time with Emily, Richard gazed at her with appreciation, and she tried not to show that she was relieved to be out of the fray. The unspoken shimmered around her. Mickey had been drinking. They were calling it an accident.

The morning of the funeral was cloud-scudded and bright. Caroline watched from a distance as Richard stood with Natalie and Emily in front of the church. Natalie wore a drop waist vintage dress made of dark green fabric and a black cloche hat. She looked as if she belonged in an English garden, drinking tea, although her choker didn't go with the dress at all. Caroline had never seen anyone look so lovely.

Natalie looked at her directly and nodded. A pulse flared in Caroline's throat. She understood that she should not mention the other night. Richard walked over and kissed her on the cheek. His warm, clean smell was familiar, and suddenly she felt sorry for him, sorry for all she could not say.

"Emily's sister wants to sit in the front row. I don't know if there's room for—" He rubbed his hand across his face.

Caroline put her hand on his arm. He seemed to have shrunk inside his clothes, his already thin frame becoming reedy. "Richard, please, put Emily's family in front. I'll sit a row or two back."

During the service, the minister spoke in measured abstractions—youth, acceptance, God's mystery. What a terrible assignment, Caroline thought, having to say all kinds of things that nobody believed. Friends glanced at her, sitting behind Richard's family, and probably imagined she was being nice or diplomatic. Nothing was further from the truth. She was not nice. Pamela had been nice—too nice. About a year after Pamela's death, Caroline had gone to see a therapist at her husband's insistence, which was surprising because Tim wasn't an introspective person, and rarely insisted on anything. The therapist made her think of an old-fashioned organ grinder. All he needed was a waxed mustache, a little monkey on a chain.

"It's the nice people, caretaker types, who get these auto-immune things," he told her.

"That doesn't sound very medical," Caroline said.

"It's not. It's just an observation."

It was true. Pamela tended to everyone around her, including her students. Bryce got his business off the ground while Pamela did the housework, made her kids' lunches, looked after them, soothed them and cheered for them, encouraged Bryce when he felt discouraged. She had been like that all through Caroline's growing up: she kept everyone else going. What was not nice about Pamela was the part of her that flirted and teased, that explained things Caroline didn't want to hear, that said to Caroline, *Do you know how to kiss? I'll show you.* The side of Pamela that was dark and provocative, the part that made Caroline most uncomfortable, that had been Pamela's true strength.

MERCIFULLY, THERE WAS NO graveside visit. A friend of Emily's had offered her house, close to the university, for a place to gather. Caroline wanted to arrive after the crowd, and she encouraged Richard to ride back with Emily. Parking at her own house, she walked the few blocks to the gathering. The bluffs, umber and orange, were shadowed by clouds. The ambiguity of Mickey's death cast them differently.

A young man who looked familiar, perhaps a former student, surveyed the improvised bar; his stance seemed temporary, as if he were merely helping himself. Caroline reached for a wine glass, then turned to find Natalie at her elbow.

"Would you like something to drink?" Caroline asked.

"Wine would be great."

Caroline poured her a large glass of Chardonnay, then poured one for herself. It felt vaguely illicit to be pouring a drink for a student, though certainly Natalie was old enough to drink.

Natalie looked at Caroline over her glass. The wine shimmered with reflected light. "Thanks for the ride home the other night."

"No problem."

They walked away from the bar together and leaned companionably in the corner. Up close, Caroline saw Natalie's dress was truly old: the neckline hand-stitched, the material sheer and unfamiliar. She guessed it was organdy.

"How's your mother?"

"Not so good." Natalie said.

Caroline studied the crowd around Emily whose hair fell smoothly to her shoulders, framing her face. She looked sleek and organized, but her expression was distraught.

"You and my father aren't terribly serious, are you?"

"No," Caroline said. "At least, I didn't plan for it to be."

"My mom thinks you're nice."

"I'm not nice," Caroline said.

"Well, you have manners."

"Exactly."

"Do you ever come to Madison?"

"Sometimes, not much." Caroline answered off-handedly, and then became aware of the sharp scent of patchouli, the closeness of Natalie standing beside her. Lulled by the wine, by the bright afternoon, she had missed the import of Natalie's question. She tried to recover. "Well, sometimes, you know. For research." Actually, she hadn't set foot in Madison's library for years. Her academic career, such as it was, had not seemed important for ages. "I'm supposed to be doing more research. I'm going to England on sabbatical next year."

"I love England," Natalie said. "I did a semester in London last year."

A whirring in her stomach made Caroline feel dizzy.

"The next time I go, I'd like to go to up to Edinburgh for the theater festival and see more of the countryside." Natalie smiled, her teeth white against her lips.

Caroline felt a pulse between her legs, a wetness, a wave of heat come over her.

Richard walked up to them and sighed. "I don't know how to deal with Mickey's friends," he said. "I don't know what to say to them."

The momentum between them was stilled. Richard's presence demanded their attention. Natalie looked as if she wanted to leave, then the thought flickered across her face like a cloud: she was the only child left. Richard stood with them for a few minutes before being drawn away to talk to someone.

At the end of the afternoon, Natalie pressed a piece of paper into Caroline's palm.

"This is my number. Call me," she said.

AFTER A WHILE, feeling blurry, Caroline excused herself. Outside, the air was warm and clear, gardens blooming, and she felt like a plant that was growing too fast: weak in the knees, wobbly and attenuated. She looked at the piece of paper. Natalie made her sevens in the European style, with little cross-hatches, like upside down £ signs. Caroline felt overcome by the fact of Natalie's handwriting on paper.

She called a few days later, saying she was coming to Madison to do some research on Saturday. Natalie suggested they meet at a Himalayan restaurant, down on State Street, for dinner.

Her voice, soft and even, made Caroline wonder, for the hundredth time, what Natalie's intention was. Did she want to talk about Richard?

On Saturday morning, Caroline debated her route. The interstate was faster, the country road through Vernon County prettier. She decided on the interstate. She'd been deliberately vague about her weekend plans with Richard, although she told herself she had nothing to feel guilty about. She was simply driving to Madison, doing some research, having dinner with his daughter, who wanted to talk. How would she describe her relationship with Richard? 'A man

I'm seeing…' *seeing* such an understatement. Richard had introduced her to his family as his 'friend' because it was polite to sidestep the sexual. 'Boyfriend' was too youthful a word, 'lover' too romantic, 'partner' inappropriate. Richard wasn't her partner, not in any real sense.

Madison was a mess of stop-and-go traffic and one-way streets. Caroline had never heard of Himalayan food, but she found the restaurant Natalie had chosen: rattan furniture, modest prices, a student place. When Caroline stepped inside, the scent of unfamiliar spices made it seem like a different country.

She looked over the menu, read it twice in great detail. After twenty minutes, she was annoyed; after forty minutes, she felt ridiculous. She tried calling Natalie, but her phone went to voicemail. Caroline didn't leave a message. What had she been thinking? She had booked a room at a small hotel, but it would be pathetic to stay. She stopped for fast food on her way out of town and took the long route home in the fading light.

BY THE TIME SHE GOT HOME, there was a message from Richard, curious about where she was, and a contrite message from Natalie, saying something about a friend and the emergency room. Caroline was ashamed to feel a vast relief. She didn't call either of them back.

She sat down in front of the television, picked up the remote, then put it down. She wouldn't go to Madison again. She would not make herself ridiculous. She would not think of Natalie's throat, her suntanned arms, the way there seemed to be a foreign city, silent, behind her eyes.

IN THE FINAL WEEKS of classes, the students were itchy. Macroeconomics didn't stand a chance against springtime. Two weeks later, Natalie called again, her voice hesitant.

"Hi," Natalie said. "I was coming home this weekend to see my mother. I wondered if you wanted to catch dinner or something. I still feel bad about standing you up."

Caroline had rehearsed this moment, how she would say no. "All right," Caroline said.

"Friday night?"

Caroline mentally ran through her appointments, trying to think if she had anything specific planned with Richard. She would rather omit the truth than have to come up with a plausible lie.

"Friday would work."

"I'm catching a ride with a friend. Can I just come by your house?"

CAROLINE WAS SUPPOSED to be grading—this final batch of papers was a ritual for departure—but she couldn't settle into a rhythm. The house needed cleaning, or dusting at least. She picked up a dust cloth, then started moving piles of books and papers. Once she got started, there was an infinite amount to do. She picked up a coffee table book on the Cotswolds—Richard had written a wistful inscription about spending time in England together. In the tumult of Mickey's death, he hadn't asked about her departure, and she hadn't offered any information. He was busy catching up on department business and other administrative chores. The lines on his face had grown deeper. He and Caroline saw each other, had dinner a few times, but hadn't slept together since Mickey's death. Now, she cleaned frantically, as if she'd drunk too much coffee, propelled by a need to keep moving.

Late in the afternoon, Caroline realized she hadn't asked Natalie what time she was coming. What was 'dinnertime' to a twenty-something? It could be ten o'clock. Years ago, when Caroline first moved to Wisconsin, she had laughed at the fact that grown-ups might eat dinner at five thirty or six o'clock. It had seemed childlike, ridiculous, but she had adjusted, mostly because of Pamela's children. By six o'clock, Caroline wondered if she would be stood up again.

Natalie appeared at seven o'clock, wearing the shirt that Caroline had first seen her in. The friend who'd dropped her off had done just that, the car was gone, as if Natalie had appeared by magic. She walked around Caroline's house, looking at her books, her photographs and knick-knacks.

"I like your house," she said. "I guessed it would be like this. You don't strike me as the subdivision type." She stopped in front of a picture of Pamela, looked at it carefully, then turned to Caroline. "When are you leaving for England?"

"Two weeks."

"Does my dad know you're leaving so soon?"

Caroline didn't feel like discussing Richard with her, and she moved toward the kitchen, gesturing that Natalie should follow. Caroline pulled a small ceramic platter down from a shelf. "You don't seem to be in final semester panic," she observed.

"This is my fifth year—I have a light semester."

"Is graduation next week?"

"I'm not really into rituals like that."

"What do you mean?"

"I don't feel like standing around, having my picture taken, wearing a stupid hat."

"Will your parents mind?"

"I don't know. Family gatherings are feeling pretty strange and sad right now."

Caroline set out dark bread and salmon, Stilton, and fruit. She opened a bottle of Chilean wine, hoped it would be all right, and they carried it all into the living room, setting it on a low table between them.

"Who's the woman in the picture?" Natalie gestured across the room.

"My sister."

"You look alike." Natalie took a slice of apple and laid a piece of cheese on top of it. "Are those her kids?" she pointed to another picture.

"Yes. Although they're not so little now: eleven and thirteen. My sister died a few years ago, and it seems odd to say, but I'm still not adjusted. Obviously, I know she's gone, but I keep thinking it's some kind of mistake."

"I don't think my brother was a mistake," Natalie said.

"You think he jumped?"

"Maybe accidentally on purpose."

Caroline nodded.

WHEN CAROLINE LOOKED at the clock, it was almost eleven. They'd never gone out for a meal; they'd opened a second bottle of wine. Alone, they talked easily, as if their pasts were two large bodies of water and their talk created a channel, an equilibrium between them.

"I've drunk too much wine to drive you anywhere," Caroline said. "Do you want to stay here? I have a guest room; it's all made up."

Natalie looked at her, red-eyed. "Yes," she said, "that would be great."

"Will your mother worry?"

"I told her I was staying with Gina, that I'd see her tomorrow."

Caroline stood up and moved toward the guest room. She shouldn't have had so much wine; it made everything confusing. Had Natalie planned to go to Gina's later or not? The ambiguity made her dizzy. Natalie followed her down the hall.

Caroline got fresh towels from the linen closet, then stopped in the shadowed hallway. The towels were a fluffy barrier between them, but she was too drunk to feel awkward. She wondered what would happen, aware that she was waiting to be kissed. For a moment, she heard a voice that sounded like Pamela's *You have to practice, you know*, and then Natalie leaned toward her, and Caroline felt herself letting go.

In the middle of the night, Caroline got up to use the bathroom, get a drink of water, and then went back to her own bed. It seemed polite, although the idea of being polite, after what they'd done, was ridiculous.

The next morning, she was filled with a quiet elation. The house was silent. Caroline showered quickly and went to the kitchen. Was Natalie accustomed to sleeping late? What if she'd risen early and left? The thought was like freezing water poured over her. The sound of footsteps padding down the hall, water running in the guest bathroom, filled Caroline with an enormous relief.

When Natalie appeared, she looked pristine and astounding.

"What do you drink in the morning?"

"Coffee," Natalie said. "Do you make it strong?"

"I do."

Caroline measured out the coffee, putting in extra, and when it was ready, they resumed their chairs from the night before. She wondered what to call this. She didn't know if Natalie would call it anything.

"What are you doing after graduation?" As soon as she asked, Caroline felt self-conscious; she sounded like an elderly aunt.

"I don't know." Natalie looked down, her dark lashes a fringe against her cheek. "I was thinking about moving to Seattle. I've got friends there. But now, with my brother gone and all, I think about my mom."

Caroline nodded. She didn't usually drink coffee first thing in the morning, but the strong coffee made her feel excited, optimistic, as if anything were possible.

"Come to England with me," Caroline said.

Natalie looked up. "Are you serious?"

Caroline's knees trembled. She felt as if her vision had grown larger, as if she could see from the corners of her eyes. "Why not? I'll have a flat in London."

Natalie looked into her cup, like a woman reading tea leaves. "Do you even know what you'd be getting into?" she murmured.

Caroline's heart thudded; she tried to take a deep breath. What would people say? What did it matter? I don't care, Caroline thought. I simply don't care.

"We have no idea what we're getting into," Caroline said. "None of us do, even when we think we do."

Natalie looked at her directly, as if wanting to see whether Caroline could hold her gaze.

"You really mean it, don't you?" Natalie's tone was a statement more than a question.

Caroline nodded, then looked out the window at the bluffs covered in mist. She didn't understand how Richard could stand to live in their shadow. She had watched them for years, loving how the light changed in each season, but they seemed harsh now, as if one false step made your choice for you.

"I'm tired of doing things halfway," Caroline said. "I've been waiting for life to get better, and suddenly that seems like a terrible mistake."

Natalie set down her cup and stretched her arms upward, the cords of her neck tightening, then turned to Caroline and grinned.

"You're sure you're up for this?" Natalie asked.

"Yes," Caroline smiled. "I am. Let's go."

Flying in the Dark

At twenty-five, I thought I had some important things figured out, which tells you how little I knew. I had a great job, a nice apartment, and after two long-term girlfriends, I had a working theory about women: I believed there was an invisible expiration date on most relationships. You know how when the milk says, 'sell by,' you wonder how many days after that it's still safe to drink? The expiration date was the tipping point between: "This is fun, what else is cool about you?" to "Where is this relationship going?" I'd learned to split up with a woman before I could be considered a jerk for stringing her along. Basically, my philosophy was bullshit.

I met Mona at a party on the Upper West Side as she was finishing a PhD in Gender Studies. Mona wrote articles about things I could barely fathom and used a vocabulary I didn't understand. A sexist might assume that someone with a degree like that would be painfully earnest, but that wasn't Mona at all. She studied pop culture, which she admitted could be humorous, and she moved through the world as if she could barely contain everything she was thinking or feeling. Mona had dark brown ringlets that fell beyond her shoulders, and everything about her was pleasingly round: her eyes and lips, her breasts, her tush, and she was sane about things that many women, in my experience, were not.

She didn't belong to a gym. She ate like a normal person. Mona never said, "Oh, I shouldn't have eaten that. I feel so fat." She had delicate hands and feet, tiny fingertips. She kept her fingernails short and bit them when she thought no one was looking.

We were at a coffee shop on the Upper West Side when Mona explained the interview process for an academic job. She drew a timeline on a napkin, explained when the job openings were announced and the various stages of the interview process. She bit her lip as she pulled a pen across the soft paper, using just the right amount of pressure to draw without ripping it. The smell of espresso and sugar swirled around me.

"The market's really tight right now. Lots of universities have Gender Studies programs, but their faculties are small. I could do a cross-appointment in English, but I'll be lucky to get anything, really."

At the napkin's edge, browned by cappuccino, Mona had drawn our potential expiration date.

"Couldn't you get a job in New York?"

"Well, a tenure-track job is pretty unlikely. You have to publish a lot, work up to it." She sounded matter-of-fact rather than aggrieved.

Being involved with a newly minted Gender Studies professor taught me this: there was no question of her sticking around to be with me. She had to do what was necessary, and I would have to figure it out.

MONA'S DESCRIPTION of looking for an academic job made me think of old-fashioned warfare—the way soldiers marched in formation, destined to be shot down. I preferred the Darwinian hustle of the business world—or I thought I did until the economy tanked, and I lost my job. Overnight, Manhattan was flooded with unemployed investment bankers—people who thought they were on the cutting edge, but found out they'd been thrashed. And Mona, after months of interviews—flying around the country to places I could barely find on a map—was offered a one-year appointment at the University of Wisconsin-La Crosse.

I was at her apartment when she got the call. Her voice sounded formal and poised as she asked questions about salary and course load. When she asked about the first day of classes, I tugged at a loose thread in the upholstery of her couch. Where the hell was La Crosse, Wisconsin? Who would name a town for a sport? Was there a Rugby, Montana?

Mona thanked the dean, or whoever she was talking to, hung up the phone, and turned to me. "You should come with me."

"To a place where people wear cheese on their heads?"

"Only on Sundays," she giggled.

She positioned herself on the opposite end of the couch, stretched her feet toward my lap and wiggled her toes. "I'm just saying, you can stay here, keep scrounging for work, or you can take a break. If you came along, well, honestly, I'd love it. I don't know anyone there, and I've got to rent a house or an apartment anyway. Doesn't your apartment cost a fortune? If you came, you could think about your game plan, look for work in Minneapolis or Madison. I don't know much about the business world, but with so many financial types looking for work, it couldn't hurt to break from the pack, could it?"

I tried to imagine telling my father, who had commuted into Manhattan every weekday for the last thirty years, that I was 'taking a break.' I couldn't remember the last time he'd taken a day off.

"It's hard to imagine leaving New York."

Mona flushed beneath her freckles. Her blush reminded me of being a kid, holding a flashlight against my hand to see the skin glow orange-pink from the light. I opened my mouth, and even before I spoke, I knew my protest was wrong. I was being a schmuck. She *had* to leave to get a job. She looked down at her hands, and the air in the room intensified around us. If I wasn't willing to leave the city, this was pretty much it.

"I kept hoping something would turn up for you here. It's hard to imagine leaving all this." I opened my hand, meaning the city outside, but sitting in Mona's narrow living room, the gesture was ridiculous.

Mona laughed. "The dirt, the traffic, the subway, the car alarms, the smell of piss in the street, baking garbage in the summer."

"It's strange to think about following you to a job."

"Women have followed men to jobs for ages," Mona said.

I WALKED HOME down Columbus Avenue. I went into a Korean market and surveyed the salad bar, the cooler, the drinks. A world of variety, but nothing I wanted. I'd been job hunting for weeks, called every headhunter I knew. Part of me knew I should stay in New York, stay in the scuffle; some of us would land decent jobs. If I asked for advice, I knew what I'd hear: my friends would tell me not to leave the city. My mother would give me advice about an engagement ring. My father would say nothing, letting me figure it out on my own.

So I did what I'd never imagined—I followed my girl-friend to her job.

ONE SATURDAY, before we left, Mona planned to go shopping for 'professor clothes' with her mother, who came by Mona's apartment with a huge bag from Zabar's, as if shopping required a particular kind of sustenance. I liked Mona's mother. She was a gynecologist, and must have explained what was what, because Mona was comfortable and relaxed and a blast in bed. Dr. Berg dressed in a style my own mother would call Upper West Side Frumpy. She wore a sack-like green dress, and her hair stood out from her head in a curly gray haze like a dandelion gone to seed.

"So, Josh, what do your parents think about you taking off for the Midwest with my daughter?" Dr. Berg fixed her diagnostician's gaze on me.

"Well, they were surprised when I told them. My father's concerned about me getting off track—job-wise—but they've met Mona, so it's easy for them to understand why I'd want to go."

"Your mother and I should have lunch at some point."

I picked up a poppyseed bagel. "Once we put you together, I'm afraid you'll be an overwhelming force."

Dr. Berg raised an eyebrow.

"My mother wants grandchildren. She's not at all subtle about it."

Mona's mother smiled. It was hard to imagine her in a room with my mother. They didn't match. My mother was a jewelry designer, and she didn't leave the house unless she was really put together—hair, nails, the whole deal. My mother could be generous and funny, but she took up a lot of air in a room. When I was a kid, I thought my father gave in to her too easily, but as I got older, I saw that he simply played his cards without drawing attention to himself.

IN AUGUST, WE MOVED to La Crosse, Wisconsin, home of the world's largest six-pack, an hour north of Prairie du Chien, which is precisely nowhere. Mona had flown out first and rented a small house near campus; when I saw what she'd rented, I couldn't believe it.

"We're *in* the 1950s" I said.

"It's like one of those Sally, Dick, and Jane books," Mona said.

La Crosse, Wisconsin, had white clapboard houses on tree-lined streets and broad strips of grass between the side-walk and the road. Tricycles and plastic shovels dotted perfect front lawns. Across the street, a little girl in a pink bathing suit ran back and forth through a sprinkler.

This fifties fantasy amazed me. What didn't exist surprised me as well: bagels, one-day dry cleaning, real ethnic food, stores open past six o'clock. Wisconsin was the whitest place I'd ever been; the place looked like an old-style L.L. Bean ad. Some of the college students had piercings or tattoos, but most of them wore no makeup, and their hair was its natural color. They rode bikes and jogged, had kayaks on their cars, wore little bracelets of colored string on their wrists.

"Everyone seems so fresh-faced."

"It's a different culture," Mona said.

And the Christian thing: people went to church every Sunday, not just the Catholics. They did something on Wednesday nights too, though we couldn't figure out what it was. Jehovah's Witnesses came to our door. SUVs sported *Promise Keeper* bumper stickers. In a little square downtown, a tombstone-shaped rock engraved with the Ten Commandments was the subject of local controversy. An iron fence around the stone, a legal attempt to make the patch of ground private property, took up a lot of editorial space in the local newspaper.

In her first week of teaching, Mona walked out the door each morning looking glossy and excited, but came home looking puzzled and upset.

"They don't talk! They actually don't speak! And you know what else? They don't know what words mean! A class of twenty year-olds! They don't know what 'ambivalence' means!" Mona tossed her satchel onto the couch. "And the bookstore—it has no books! They sell mugs and sweatpants, but they have 'textbook rental.' It sounds like a bargain for the students, and I suppose it's fine for anatomy or something, I mean, our bones don't change, right? But some of the professors have been using the same books for *years!* And get this: since I asked the students to *buy* books, I was supposed to put a disclaimer in the course catalog, telling students they might have to spend more than forty-five dollars on books."

"Wouldn't that help you get some serious students?"

Mona flopped down on a chair. "Well, I hope so, but if my courses don't fill, I'm out of a job."

Mona did like the Women's Studies professors—and there were a few students with inquiring minds—but most days she came home looking beaten, and it was clear that teaching wasn't going the way she planned.

SINCE MONA'S JOB was a one-year appointment, we didn't want to spend much money on setting up the house, so we lived with furniture that could only be called ironic—the local secondhand stores did a big business in seventies lamps and vinyl furniture. To me, it felt like an exotic experiment in American culture, but I couldn't say this aloud because, career-wise, it wasn't experimental for Mona at all.

I learned how old-fashioned housewives must have felt. I could easily fill my time—I went running on the trails beneath the bluffs, showered, updated LinkedIn, checked my email, applied for consulting gigs, followed up with phone calls—but waiting for Mona to come home was the undercurrent of my day.

As we settled into a campy domesticity, I got a little project work. A friend had done a consulting job for the Western Wisconsin Power Cooperative, which had a large plant on the Mississippi, just south of La Crosse. Marshall's firm had crunched some numbers for different alternative energy scenarios, and because I'd worked for him on another project, I knew enough to field client questions and help them consider different directions they might take. It was consulting hand-holding, but good PR for his company; his team was sick of flying to Wisconsin.

LIVING IN LA CROSSE with Mona felt like a strange outpost. Mona herself was real and necessary, but the backdrop of our lives was bizarre. Our neighbors had a red Chevy pickup with a decal: *Bite me, Ford-boy.* I stared at it one afternoon as I drank a cup of coffee, then went down to the basement to put some laundry in the dryer. As I reached into the washing machine to pull a damp sock off the side, the sock moved, chirped, and tried to unfurl a stick-like wing. I jumped back, then peered inside. A bat. Two, actually. One was brown smush on the bottom, a casualty of the spin cycle.

I closed the lid. At home, you called someone: a super, a handyman, an eccentric neighbor, but in the land of do-it-yourself, it wasn't always obvious who to call. I walked upstairs to find Mona.

She was puzzling over a student paper, hands gripping her dark curls in a posture I had come to recognize: trying to keep her head on straight when confronted with colossal ignorance.

"Josh, this student believes that Zora Neale Hurston was alive during the Civil War! That the Civil War took place in 1940!"

I tried to show the appropriate look of shock and surprise. I had the big events in American history pretty well covered, but Zora with-two-last-names escaped me. From Mona's tone, it was clear I was supposed to know.

"There's a bat in the washing machine."

"What?"

"And I think another one that's dead."

Mona's skin went white beneath her freckles.

"Do bats get rabies?" she asked.

"I don't know."

"Let's call the landlord," Mona said. She dug through a basket of papers on her desk, but when she tried to call, he wasn't home.

I reached for the phone book, which wasn't even an inch thick with the white and yellow pages combined. I found *Animal Control* and was surprised when a woman, rather than a machine, answered. I explained what I'd found in the washer.

"Do you know how to deal with bats?" she asked.

"Well, no. That's why I'm calling. We're wondering if a bat can get rabies."

"Is the bat acting peculiar?"

"I don't know how bats usually act."

"Give me your address."

TWENTY MINUTES LATER, a stocky woman in a cigar-colored uniform appeared at our door. She held a large metal Maxwell House can and a stick with a bright orange net.

"It's in the washing machine," I said.

Mona hung back by the stairs, her hands by the sides of her face.

The woman followed me into the basement. She put on a pair of thick leather gloves, opened the washing machine, and reached in for the dead bat on the bottom. She scooped it into the container, then bent to examine the bat on the side more closely. Gently, she closed her hand around the bat, which didn't seem to resist, and set it in the container, snapping on the lid. A few faint thumps, then it stopped. I felt ridiculous that I hadn't done this myself.

"Do you have any pets it could have bitten before it got into the machine?"

"No."

"Did you touch it?"

"No, it moved as I was reaching for it."

"Well, we'll test it for rabies anyway—we had a few cases last year. Let's go upstairs and I'll get your information."

We all went up to the living room, where the woman sat down in our ugly armchair covered with brown and orange flowers. It was the only piece of furniture that was truly comfortable. When she set the container on the floor, Mona eyed it suspiciously.

"How did it get into our washing machine?" Mona asked.

"Well, a bat can get through an opening as small as 3/8 of an inch, which is about the diameter of a dime. They can get through cracks in the siding, dryer vents, old chimneys. Sometimes, in winter, when we get a warm spell like this, they come out of hibernation, looking for water, and get a little lost. You could also have a maternity colony in your attic or in the walls. You'd hear them."

"What does it sound like?"

"It's a little ticking, a scratching noise, inside the wall."

Mona's eyes and mouth grew round. "Oh, god, I've heard that the past few days!"

"Let me give you some information." She handed Mona a flyer prepared by the Wisconsin DNR, which was clearly for people like us because I could make out the words DON'T PANIC on the front.

I HOPED OUR BAT episode was an isolated incident, but one Saturday night, after we'd been out to dinner, and debated whether deep-fried cheese curds were a real menu item, or a heart-stopping tourist joke, Mona ran into the living room.

"Upstairs! Another bat!"

I'd read the flyer—we were supposed to open a door or window and let the bat fly out. Mona ran into the bathroom and locked the door. I headed upstairs.

The bat, trilling loudly, darted back and forth across the bedroom. It moved surprisingly quickly in the small space. A rush of anxiety blew through me, blood beat in my ears, and I hurried over to the window and tried to push it open. The window stuck. For a moment, I couldn't hear the bat. What if it landed on my back? I pushed harder—the window had been shut all winter—and finally the sash flew up with a bang. My fingers shook as I fumbled with the corroded screen releases. The bat trilled behind me. The releases wouldn't give, and I punched them with side of my fist. When they finally came loose, the screen fell from the window, a flimsy clattering, two stories down.

The bat dipped back and forth. I ducked out of the bedroom, closing the door behind me.

"Did you get it?" Mona peeked out from behind the bathroom door.

"I opened the window. I figured it'd be easiest if I got out of the way."

Mona came out into the living room. She sat hunched on the couch, hands pressed between her knees.

"I read the paperwork the animal control woman left," I said. "We're not actually supposed to let it loose in the cold, it'll probably freeze to death. We're supposed to catch it and let it loose in the basement or the attic, so it can go back to hibernating."

"Screw that," Mona said.

I knew better than to invoke any of the eco-feminist speak I'd heard from Mona's friends and, after a decent interval, I went upstairs to see if it was gone. Opening the door, I scanned the walls and corners. Nothing. Cold air filled the room.

"Mona! The coast is clear," I called.

We were getting undressed when the bat darted across the room. Mona, naked, screamed and dove for the covers. I was distracted for a moment, watching her, but she pulled the covers over her.

I ran to the window, pushed it open again, then pulled on my sweatpants. Mona yelled from under the covers, "Get it out! Get it out!"

"Mona, be quiet! You're freaking the thing out!"

The bat's chirping, high and loud, echoed against the low, slanted ceilings. It dove back and forth; blood pounded in my head. I picked up my sweatshirt and swatted it. The bat tangled in the thick cotton, and I shoved the sweatshirt out the window. The angry trilling stilled.

"Mona, you can come out now."

"Why was it still in here?" Her voice was tearful.

"It must have been resting."

"It's gone now?"

"It's gone."

THE NEXT MORNING, after Mona left for teaching, I went out to the side yard to retrieve the screen. I picked up my sweatshirt, shook it, and the bat fell to the ground. Its brown fur, tinged with soft orange, seemed a strange contrast to its wide-open mouth with tiny, sharp teeth. I gently pulled on the edges of its wings; its wingspan was more than a foot across.

WHEN DR. BERG CALLED MONA, I pretended to be occupied while I listened to Mona describe our bat problem. These conversations morphed into her doubts about her job, the unpreparedness of her students, the pettiness of academic politics. Although Mona only had a one-year appointment, it turned out that her contract could be extended. The idea did not excite me. I studied the bat pamphlet.

Bat Fact #1
Bats will *not* fly into our hair

Mona had studied the bat literature, and when she finally reached the landlord, she insisted he come over and find the places where a bat could get in. When he came by the house, he had a neat gray mustache and a cardigan like Mr. Rogers.

"Yah, it'll happen. You just have to open a door or window, shoo them out."

Mona looked stunned. "We can't live like that!"

"Can't exclude them this time of year. If you cover holes to the outside, they look for a way out through the inside, and you get even more of them in the house. Or else they die in the attic, which would give you a bad smell. Just how it is, they come with the territory."

LATE ONE AFTERNOON, we sat in the People's Food Co-op, drinking coffee. Watching people walk by, we could pretend we were in a city.

"I thought academic politics were mainly at the more prestigious places, but it's just brutal here." Mona described a scenario that I tuned out slightly. Across the street, a crane set a beam on top of a new building. I tuned back in when I heard a change in her voice, something about a trip to Pittsburgh. "So, I could go to the conference at Carnegie Mellon, and you could come along and do whatever you felt like in Pittsburgh. I don't need to attend every session."

"Sure," I said. "Let's go."

WE HEARD THEM in the walls at night, a tiny scritching sound that wouldn't keep you awake—unless you knew it was bats. We'd have a few quiet days, tell ourselves it was over, and then a bat would turn up inside the house. There'd been a warm streak in February, and I kept hoping for cold so the bats would freeze back into hibernation.

I was watching basketball one night when Mona hurried out of the bathroom, squealing and pulling up her pants.

"It's on the wall!" She mouthed as if the bat would hear her.

I poked my head into the bathroom. The bat was near the ceiling, hanging upside-down.

"Okay, get a piece of cardboard—a cereal box or something."

"I can't!"

"Go get some cardboard."

"It freaks me out!"

I had a large, plastic yogurt container ready. I handed her the container and carried a chair into the bathroom, setting it quietly on the floor so I wouldn't wake the bat. I took the container, stepped onto the chair, and quickly set the container over the bat, which trilled angrily, banging against the thin plastic.

"Hand me the cardboard. I'm going to lift the container away from the wall just a little bit."

"No! Don't let it out."

"Don't be ridiculous, I won't."

"I can't!"

"Mona, I can't stand here forever." The bat thudded against the container; I felt its small weight against my hand.

Mona handed me the cardboard, and I lifted one side of the container away from the wall and shoved the cardboard forward. It met with resistance, the body of the bat, squealing like mad.

I slid the cardboard all the way through, then turned the container upright, holding the cardboard on top. Triumph. The bat chirped, high and insistent. Stepping down off the chair, I stumbled but held the container upright. Mona screamed.

"Mona, enough." I walked toward the front door, and she ran ahead of me to open it.

"Take it far away, so it won't come back!"

"Mona, it's February. I don't have any shoes on."

I held the container toward her, but she stepped back, putting up her hands.

"Okay, help me with my shoes."

She reached for my sneakers, pulling them open the way she might for a child, putting her finger in the back so I could slide my foot in. With the shoelaces undone, I stepped out into the night. The bat thumped.

It was freezing outside, and I wondered how far I had to go so it wouldn't head back to the house. My guess was that bats had pretty good homing instincts, and that, even if I walked a mile, it would be back. I shuffled up the street, the air cold on my chest and arms, and wondered how to let it loose without having it fly up at me. The sky was thick with stars, some so bright I wondered if they were satellites, others were tiny pricks of light. I could actually see the Milky Way. I stood for a moment, gazing up. I had never seen the real thing before—a pale edgeless road in the sky. Walking down to the end of the block, I set the container down, tipped it over, and stepped back. The bat lay still, stunned, then flitted into the air.

THE NEXT MORNING, Mona went off to teach her Women's Studies seminar, a class with upper-level students that she looked forward to. She threw her backpack over her shoulder and reached back, pulling her curls out from under the strap. Between the bats and her recalcitrant students, Mona said she had demoted herself to her backpack; she didn't feel like a professor.

"Is there someone else we can call? If the landlord won't fix it, I'll pay for it myself. Will you see what you can do?"

"I'll try, Mona."

She nodded and slipped out the door.

I sat in the quiet, surveying our meager house. I didn't mind that she had essentially dumped this problem in my lap, I did have more time, but last week I'd turned down some work in Minneapolis because Mona didn't want to be left alone with the bats. We had to find a better way.

I turned to the phone book again and looked under *Bats*. Nothing. I tried *Pest Control* and found ads for exterminating bees, carpenter ants, termites, and there in tiny letters: Wisconsin Bat Specialist.

A few hours later, a cheerful man in a ball cap showed up at our door. He tromped around the house in the melted snow and pointed out places where bats were getting in.

He showed me tell-tale droppings on the side of the house and explained that bat droppings had bits of shiny material, insects, in them. No white, like bird droppings. He said the bluffs on both sides of the Mississippi were one reason there were so many bats here. He claimed bats were helpful because they ate mosquitoes, which caused encephalitis, West Nile Virus, and all those other scary things we heard about in the news. So bats were environmentally important and shouldn't be killed. He confirmed what our landlord had said: he couldn't exclude them until August. He advised me to get a butterfly net at Fleet Farm. He said it was easier to catch them if you snuck up behind them.

WHEN MONA CAME HOME, and I explained what the man had said, she drooped.

"It's inhumane to kill them?"

"Inhumane, politically incorrect, environmentally unfriendly. The whole deal."

"And we can't get rid of them?"

"They're in the walls and attic. Apparently quite a lot of them. There's nothing he can do until late summer."

"I can't wait to go to Pittsburgh. Just to stay in a hotel and not have any surprises." Mona sat down in our ugly armchair and looked as if she were going to cry.

ON THE WAY TO PITTSBURGH, I tried to pay attention to the point of this conference. Mona was presenting a paper on Chris Bohjalian's *Trans-Sister Radio*: Gender and something. Academics had to have colons in the titles of their papers, this much, I knew. A grad school friend of hers would pick us up at the airport.

When we arrived, a skinny woman with short dark hair, wearing black clothes and clunky shoes, lounged outside the Baggage Claim. Audrey looked like a weary punk rocker; she threw an arm around Mona's neck and hugged her, then we carried our bags to her beat-out Celica. Audrey pulled out of the airport like a NASCAR driver.

"Guess what happened to me in class the other day?" Mona said.

"What?" Audrey shot past an old Mercedes.

"I'm teaching an Intro class called *Power, Privilege, and Gender*. I've got this girl in class who, no matter what the assignment is, turns in papers with Bible quotes, saying how homosexuality is an abomination. We've talked about tolerance, about Matthew Shepherd, the whole deal, so the last time she did it, I failed her paper. When I gave the papers back, she put her head down on her desk. I thought she was crying. I have this other student who's pretty cool, and she said, "She's praying for you.""

"No!"

"Yes, it was true. She was praying for my soul."

"You've got to get out of there," Audrey said.

"But isn't that the point of teaching? To try to educate people?"

"They have to be willing to learn," Audrey said.

Outside, the landscape was muddy and barren. I'd expected more suburban sprawl outside of Pittsburgh. As we sped towards a large tunnel, Audrey glanced back at me. "Ever been to Pittsburgh?"

"No," I said.

"Well, check out the view when we come out of the tunnel."

I thought of the West Side Drive: the Cloisters, the George Washington Bridge, the broad Hudson. I prepared myself for something underwhelming. We sped through the tunnel, and when we came out, high above Pittsburgh, the city and river and bridges were wide and vast and shining. Without leaves on the trees, we could see the bones of the cityscape, the variegated grays and glints of green. I felt a thrill, as if coming back to life.

In Pittsburgh, we ate Thai food, Japanese food, Greek food. We drank Thai beer, and sake and wine. We kept ending up in bed. Mona gave her paper but hardly went to any of the conference.

On our third day in Pittsburgh, we lay back in bed, sweating.

"Is it possible to come without moving?" Mona languid, brushed her hair out of her face.

"I don't know, let's see," I said.

Mona rolled toward me, her hair falling past her shoulders, onto my chest. "It's such a relief not to worry about some flying rat appearing out of nowhere."

I kissed her shoulder, the skin pale and glistening.

"I'm glad you came with me," she said.

"I was glad to get out of La Crosse."

"No, I meant with me, to the job."

"It didn't cost me anything," I said.

She sat up and pulled the sheet in front of her, looking at me hard.

"No, not like that. I wanted to be with you. I just mean it would be wrong to act like it was this big sacrifice."

She nodded.

"There's one thing though." I knew I should shut my mouth, but I had to say it. "You have all these feminist theories, you think about the gender implications of politics, advertising, all that. But you have to admit—you're as capable of catching a bat as I am—but you leave it to me because you know I'll do it."

Mona looked angry for a moment, clouds passing over her face, then smiled.

"Gender expectations are unfair. I've taken advantage of your prescribed role." She grinned, a little wickedly. "I admit it, you're right, but I'm telling you I just can't do it. I'll keep playing on all those traditional manly attributes."

And I kissed her, really just wanting her to admit I had a point.

WHEN I HEARD MONA SCREAM, I didn't have to ask. A bat darted through the kitchen, and Mona ran upstairs, slamming the bedroom door behind her.

I was tired. I really just wanted to chill out and look at stupid stuff online. I shut my laptop, and got up to open the back door, then the front, hoping the bat would find its way out, but the currents of cold spring air seemed to confuse it, and the bat dipped in and out of the kitchen. I was sick of this constant interruption. I was homesick for New York. I picked up the kitchen broom, and as the bat flew toward me, I nailed it.

WHEN MONA CAME BACK from school the next day, the two vertical lines inside her eyebrows looked deeper. She chewed on the side of her thumb.

"What's up?"

"They offered me a three-year contract." She set down her backpack and sank into the armchair.

I tried to think of the right thing to say. "It's not tenure-track, though."

"No, it's not."

I took her hand and pulled her over to the couch; she shuffled her feet like a child. "What do you want to do?" I asked.

"Well, I should take it. It's the smart thing to do. But I hate it here. The students don't want to discuss things! They don't argue!"

"You've said yourself it's a cultural thing. I think we belong somewhere more urban—like Pittsburgh."

"You can't just choose a city—you have to cast a wide net."

"So go on the job market again. It's always easier to get a job when you have one."

She sniffed. "I suppose so."

"What's wrong?"

"Nothing's working out the way I thought. I thought I'd be a professor, and the students would talk, and be interested in ideas. I thought…" Mona started to hiccup. "I thought they'd *like* me." She started to cry.

"Mona, I can't imagine anyone not liking you," I whispered into her hair. I let her cry for a few minutes, then felt myself gathering for it, what I'd been thinking for weeks.

"They don't. They actually *don't* like me. I piss them off." Her voice was muffled.

Nervousness welled in my throat; I swallowed it back. "Mona, you're astounding. If they don't get it, that's on them. Mona, look at me."

"What?" She sat up. The tip of her nose was red; tears ran down to her mouth.

"Mona, please marry me." I held her hand. My pulse pounded in my head. I'd thought it, but I'd planned to get a ring, to do it right.

"You're not kidding, are you?"

"Of course not." I looked at her, steadily. She looked beautiful and tearful and astonished all at once.

Mona gave a trembling smile.

"My mother will kill me for proposing without a ring. We'll shop for one at home, okay?" My throat was dry. I should have bought the ring first. "Listen, this place wasn't a good fit for you, but you'll find something. We can do anything we want."

"It's a big step." She smiled and leaned into me.

I knew she would say yes.

Sitting there, with Mona beside me, I thought of driving into Pittsburgh—how one minute we were in a tunnel, in the dark, and I'd steeled myself for nothing special, and the next minute the city and river and bridges opened before us. From a distance, we couldn't see the intricacies below, but driving in, moving closer, we came down to street level and became part of the city's life: crowds of people hurrying down the sidewalk, the smell of coffee and steam and tar, bright shards of conversation in languages I didn't understand, the grit of bright murals and chipped paint. We joined the bark and pulse of the city, joined everything we were heading for that we couldn't completely see.

IV

Look Both Ways

The buses all looked the same in the dark. Kevin squinted through the snow at the open belly door, like a dragon's stomach, where the others had piled their gear to be stowed. That girl with the insane pom-pom hat—what was her name? she was everywhere—darted through the crowd and climbed onto the bus. This must be the one.

He dropped his snowboard, boots, and duffle bag at the edge of the pile—oh, he had to piss, there were bathrooms on the bus, right?—and, fumbling for his pack, he moved towards the door. His foot pawed the air. He grabbed the handrail and tried again. Good. Just wasted enough. Leaving Colorado at dusk, by morning he'd be halfway to Nashville, back to Vandy, well not back to Vandy as it turned out, but back to . . . something.

Grabbing the seat tops, Kevin wobbled toward the back. He dropped his pack on an empty seat and made his way to the bathroom. The watery light made everything greenish, oh this ride was going to be brutal, and then, relieved, he wobbled up the aisle, searching for the reflective tape on his pack.

The bus filled. Hopefully, Jason would show up soon and snag the seat next to him. Kevin settled in and closed his eyes.

It didn't matter. Nothing mattered, really. This was the Zen state he'd been aiming for. After complaining about school for the past year—how Vanderbilt was full of privileged snotty nobs, how he had no idea what he wanted to study, so why was he in school anyway?—his tuition waiver had been revoked for something he never could have predicted: his mother, an anesthesiologist on the teaching faculty, had been intervened on—packed off to rehab for prescription drugs, and while she was "on leave," his tuition waiver did not apply. His *mother*. His beige, uptight mother. Of course, he'd seen her unhinged, mainly at him. His DUI last year had been a real tearfest, but he couldn't get over his mother getting in trouble, getting caught.

Everything blew up before Christmas. He'd already paid for the Ski Club trip, so they let him go, but without the tuition break, his father didn't want to pay for a semester at Vanderbilt, and since Kevin wasn't enrolled, he couldn't live in the dorm, so everything unraveled pretty damn quickly. His mother was in rehab for three months. Minimum. Three fucking months. He hadn't visited yet, and his older sister, usually his ally, had been blunt on Christmas Eve.

"You know, the whole troubled teen thing really stressed them. Don't you think you're done playing that card? Don't you think you've been an asshole long enough?"

Harsh. He swirled eggnog in a tumbler. Breakfast, dessert, and alcohol all in one viscous package; the opacity was kind of gross. Thinking of it now made him queasy. He pressed his coat against the window and went to sleep.

He woke in the dark, thirsty, and pulled out his phone. 6:43 a.m. Shit. A text from Jason: Where r u? Kevin sat up, looked around, but couldn't see him. He closed his eyes. Oh, he needed water. Next to him, a guy in a navy parka stirred, half-opened a crusty eye, and looked out.

"Where are we?" Kevin asked.

"Nebraska. It's always Nebraska."

His accent sounded Russian, but Kevin couldn't tell if it was real or a joke. "Funny dude."

"The American tundra."

Kevin tried to picture a map of the United States. A hot fear started in his stomach and moved towards his bowels. He sat up, straighter, and looked around the bus. No one looked familiar. Tingling waves ran out to the rest of his body, and he remembered the night he'd gotten his DUI, the glare of the police station, the molten shame that he'd done something he couldn't take back. Across the aisle, a girl wore a purple sweatshirt. Winona State. He smirked. It wasn't spelled right. A row ahead, and on the other side, someone else wore a purple sweatshirt. Could he have gotten on the wrong bus? Oh, not possible.

LATER IN THE MORNING, after they had stopped for gas and started up again, after he had subtly confirmed for himself that yes, he was on the wrong bus, and no, Winona was not spelled Wynona, like Judd or Ryder, that he was going to somewhere else, he had to ask his seatmate.

"Hey, where exactly is Winona State?"

The boy looked at him without expression, turning up one corner of his mouth. "You got on the wrong bus?"

"Yeah, but I don't want them to drop me off in the middle of nowhere, so don't say anything, okay?"

"Where were you going back to?"

"Tennessee. Nashville."

The boy put his head against the seat in front of him, wheezing with suppressed laughter. When he sat up, he smiled and wiped his eyes.

"Idiot. When I came to this country, my father and I landed at the Minneapolis airport, got a taxi, and my father said, 'Take us to the Russian neighborhood in Minneapolis.' The driver looked at us like we were crazy. He said, 'There is no Russian neighborhood. Where do you want to go?'"

Kevin sat back. "So, I'm screwed, but really, where are we going?"

"Minnesota."

"Shit."

"Not really. I come from Siberia. You want to talk shit? That's some shit."

Outside, miles of corn stubble poked through the snow. He had maybe twenty-five dollars left. No credit card. What could he do? Call his dad and ask for a plane ticket? It seemed ridiculous, even for him.

He'd always imagined that, after he was done screwing up, his parents would be there, waiting for him. When he got his head together, it would seem as if he'd come through a passage, that he'd still be himself, but he'd join the world of people who knew what they were doing.

After the DUI, his mother insisted he go see a therapist. It became a condition of living in the dorm rather than at home, and he figured he could bullshit his way through fifty minutes a week if it bought him a little freedom. It reminded him of being a kid, when he'd had to see the school counselor because his mom had put him on drugs for ADD, or ADHD, or whatever they were calling it then.

This time, the therapist, Mark Something, was a nice guy, low-key, but Kevin didn't feel like talking. He sounded witless, even to himself. He tried to play the accident down, but it had scared him. He'd crashed into a stop sign, flattened it, and as he told this to the therapist, the irony of it was too much.

Mark tapped a pencil on his pad.

"What was your father's response?"

"My mother's the one who's so damn overwrought."

"That may be true, but I'm curious: how did he react?"

"He barely reacts to anything. He's an engineer at heart. He works at 3M. My mom's like a spastic whippet. If you made her stand still, she'd screw herself into the ground. And my dad basically pacifies her by agreeing with her. Sometimes I wish he'd man up and put his foot down, or get pissed off, but he pretty much goes along."

"Do you think you're trying to provoke a reaction from him?"

"Jeezus—no." Kevin picked up a small ceramic elephant resting on a table near his chair; the figure was handmade, kind of impressionistic. "I just wish he'd just tell my mother to take a breath. She's constantly vigilant, Mad-Eye Moody, you know?"

The therapist drew his eyebrows together. "I don't get the reference."

Kevin set the elephant down. "He was a character in those *Harry Potter* books. His motto was 'Constant Vigilance!' That's my mother. She's exhausting."

THE BUS CHANGED GEARS and slowed, a twenty-minute stop for food and coffee. What could he do? He couldn't afford a hotel. He could ask his seatmate about crashing at his place, but Boris, or whatever his name was, didn't seem too friendly.

The gas station smelled like old hot dogs; the coffee would be terrible, so he ordered hot chocolate. When he turned around, the pom-pom girl, her red pom-pom flattened, was behind him. She ordered a cup of tea.

"Hey," Kevin said.

"Hi."

"If I tell you a secret, you promise you won't bust me?"

She had a round face, wind-burned cheeks. She seemed like the kind of person you could trust to babysit.

"Sure, why not?"

"I got on the wrong bus. I was supposed to be going back to Nashville, but instead I'm going… I don't know… wherever this bus is going."

She giggled. "Seriously?"

"Yeah. Is there a hostel, or any place that's cheap to stay in Winona?"

"I don't know of any." She shook her head. "I don't think so."

It frightened him, how quickly she answered.

They walked over to the counter for milk and sugar, and she chose a wooden stick to stir her tea. "Are you a jerk or an axe murderer or something?"

"No. Well, maybe a jerk sometimes, but not on purpose."

"What kind of jerkdom?"

He wondered where he should draw the line. "Well, I've changed my major at least three times in two years, I don't always remember to put the toilet seat down, I'm kind of unconscious about my surroundings…"

"Obviously."

He smiled. He felt ridiculous standing there, hoping his presence might invite help.

"My housemates are gone over the break, and one of them has a brother who's staying in her room for a week. You could crash on our couch for a few days, but if you eat my groceries, or you're weird, he'll hurt you. He's actually very sweet, but he's one of those CrossFit guys. He could beat the crap out of you without even trying."

Kevin took a deep breath. "No one will need to keep me line, but I'd really appreciate the couch. What's your name?"

"Tabitha."

He took a sip of hot chocolate. "Cool name."

"My mother liked the show *Bewitched*."

Kevin mentally scrolled through images from *Nick at Night*. "The show where the woman wiggles her nose to get stuff done?"

"That's it."

"You're named for someone with magical powers."

Tabitha nodded towards the door. "We should get back on. This'll be our last stop. I'll look for you when we get off."

WHEN THEY GOT OFF the bus and collected their luggage, it was morning, but the day felt fuzzy and distended. They lugged their gear to a boxy house near campus. In the living room, she pointed to a brown, corduroy-covered couch. "That's you," she said. A short man with a bushy beard emerged, looking as if he'd just gotten out of the shower. His crumpled ears were small; his biceps filled his shirt sleeves. He nodded to Kevin, who stretched out on the sofa, used his coat as a blanket, and went to sleep.

WHEN HE WOKE, it was afternoon, and he lay still, trying to think of what to do. He didn't want to call his dad, who'd probably say: *get a job, work your way home.* Kevin called Melissa.

"Hey, 'sup?"

"Sup? Snowboarding made you all gangsta now?"

"Hardly."

"How was the trip?"

"Well, it's not quite over."

Melissa waited.

"I got on the wrong bus coming home."

"What? Where are you?"

"Minnesota."

Melissa laughed.

"I seem to be providing a lot of amusement for people. But yeah, I'm here in the frozen north, and I'm broke. A girl is letting me crash on her couch—but I've got to get cash to get home. I haven't called Dad yet."

"It won't do you much good. He went to Puerto Rico."

"What?"

"Apparently, he and Mom made plans months ago, and he's been to see her a few times, and she told him he might as well go."

"Jeez."

"I was kind of worried about him with Mom gone, and when I called him, he said he'd decided to get away. Apparently, he needs to do some thinking."

"Did he say that?"

"Not exactly, but that was what he implied. Anyway, good luck reaching him—he's not exactly responsive. And I don't have a couple hundred dollars to spare."

Kevin picked at a bare spot on the couch. "What's it like . . . seeing Mom?"

"It's weird. You have to be on a list to get in."

"Exclusive."

"No, you have to be approved so that people don't put their dealers on the list."

"Damn."

"I know. I guess the whole addiction thing with anesthetists and anesthesiologists is tricky. They basically have to do super rehab. And I talked to Dad after you left—Mom'll be pissing in a cup until she retires—and that's the best-case scenario. They can prosecute her. Each thing she's taken could be a separate charge. Can you imagine Mom in jail?"

Both of them were silent. His mother always left a gleaming kitchen before she maneuvered her Saab out of the garage. A peace settled on the house when she was gone.

"We're like a flashback in *Orange is the New Black*," Kevin said.

Melissa hiccupped; he'd gone too far.

"Poor Mom, is she having a hard time?"

"Of course she is! It's rehab. She has to deal with all the stuff she's spent her life repressing."

The world pressing in. He knew the feeling. "Well, I'll try to sell my snowboard and my boots. Seriously though, can I hit you up for food money? I can't mooch off this girl who's letting me stay at her place."

"Text me and I'll figure something out."

"Thanks, Melly." He set down his phone.

Outside, the afternoon light deepened, becoming granular. His stomach gnawed. He needed a shower. In the bathroom, she'd set out a towel with a note: *Here—*. Funny girl.

After a shower, he felt better. He dressed, slipped his computer into his pack, and stepped outside.

Wind riffled at his neck. He pulled his hat over damp hair. The cold wasn't too bad. Tabitha had pointed in the direction of downtown: over the railroad tracks and towards the river. A spindly kid stood at the crosswalk.

"Food and coffee? Wi-fi?" Kevin asked.

"Acoustic Café. It's a few blocks down there." The kid pointed with an oversized glove.

WHEN KEVIN WALKED in the door, the smell of deli sandwiches hit him like a wave. He ordered coffee and a turkey sub with everything on it. The café had heavy dark furniture, windows that looked onto the street, and clumsy artwork on the walls. While the cashier rang up his sandwich, he studied a poster: *Frozen River Film Festival*. February. Hopefully, he wouldn't still be here. The cashier gave him a number, and he settled into a booth.

Kevin flipped open his laptop. Was this town big enough for Craigslist? Probably not. Maybe someplace in town would buy used equipment.

He searched for flights to Nashville, but they were expensive. Even if he found a job, he'd have to work for almost a month to buy a ticket. And a shuttle to the Minneapolis airport cost $50. He punched in *Greyhound,* but when he tried Winona and Nashville, the options wouldn't load. A girl with curly red hair brought his sandwich, and he pushed his computer aside. The bread was soft and warm, and the sandwich, with some kind of dressing and yellow banana peppers, was amazing. Online, he searched for used equipment stores, sports stores, pawn shops, any place that might buy his gear.

He drank his coffee and debated buying another sandwich, but he needed to save money for tomorrow; he picked up the last bits of lettuce and dressing, then headed out to the street.

Second-hand stores, gift shops, a law office, a bank with ornate stained-glass windows, an acupuncturist, outdoor store, no, it was the pawn shop. He pushed open the door. Guns & DVDs. Camo jackets and fishing poles. He walked up to the counter where two guys talking to each other ignored him.

By the cash register, a stuffed squirrel, a real one, perched on its hind legs grabbing its little squirrel balls; its tiny mouth was open. Kevin snorted.

"Yeah?" A guy in a feed cap looked over at him.

"Do you guys take snowboards, boots, stuff like that?"

"Not really, no."

Kevin walked out into the street. He passed a yarn store, a hairdresser, a veterinary clinic. He turned a corner: Adventure Ski & Cycle. When he pushed open the door, the smell of new tires washed over him. At the counter, a guy with a huge brown beard peered over his glasses at his phone.

"Do you buy used equipment?"

"We buy used bikes, that's about it."

"No used snowboards, boots, that kind of thing?"

"No, we rent skis though."

Back outside, it was getting dark.

THE NEXT DAY, he headed in the opposite direction. He passed a store called Sole Sports, but it had high-end gear; they wouldn't buy used stuff. He passed a credit union, industrial buildings, a used clothing store, then saw a sign: Winona Food Shelf. He stopped in the cold. He could just go in, see what they had. As he stood, watching his breath plume in the air, a woman parked a beat-out Chrysler in front; she helped a kid out of a car seat in back while an older kid in a thin coat climbed out by herself. No, no way, he'd be embarrassed to go in when other people needed it more.

He walked for what felt like miles. At the end of the bus ride the other day, he'd seen a Target, a Walgreens, and other box stores; he wondered if they were hiring. How much was minimum wage here? He calculated what he could raise by selling his gear and how much he'd make by working. He didn't want Tabitha's roommates to come back and be pissed that he was crashing there. Finally, he came to the edge of a parking lot: Walmart, Target, a place called Fleet Farm. In Target, he asked if they were hiring.

"In a few weeks. You can fill out an application online."

He tried Walmart, a fitness store, a liquor store. Clearly, this was the wrong time to look for work. Hibernation mode, no one was hiring.

He'd always had money from lifeguarding in the summer and selling the Adderall he'd stopped using. Selling the Addy was pocket change, really, but he'd never needed much. His stomach knotted in on itself. He saw a McDonald's across the highway, but even that wasn't cheap. The sky was growing deep gray, and snippets of conversation swirled around him: *looks like snow, yep, it's coming.*

He went back into Target and walked to the grocery section. He pretended to shop while he looked around for stockers. He unzipped his coat a little and, standing in front of the granola bars, he waited for some girls to roll their cart into the next aisle. Glancing in both directions, he grabbed a box and stuffed it in his coat.

Moving down the aisle, he felt for the top of the box. He ripped the tab, pulled out a granola bar, palmed it, and walked over toward Electronics. He pretended to study the headphones while he opened the wrapper. Fake strawberry. He ate four bars, walked over to Sporting Goods, pulled the last two bars out of the box, then quickly stuffed the empty box behind a display of yoga mats. Feeling a little sick, he went outside for air.

DARK AND WIND BLEW off the lake. He hoped he could get back to Tabitha's. He was heading in the right direction, but all the tiny houses looked the same. He texted Tabitha to get her address, and luckily, he wasn't too far off. He felt as if he'd walked all day.

The smell of spaghetti sauce greeted him when he opened the door.

"Hi there," Tabitha called from the kitchen.

"Hey."

"Want some spaghetti?"

"That'd be great."

Tabitha swirled a little water in the jar to get the last bit of sauce, then dumped it into the saucepan.

"You want any help?"

"Nah"

"Didn't have much luck selling my gear."

Tabitha puckered her lips. "Did you try that bike & ski place in town?"

"Yeah."

"There's a Stuff for Sale in Winona Facebook page. I've never tried it, but friends of mine have bought stuff off it."

"I'll try it." He didn't want to say he'd asked about jobs, because he didn't want her to think she'd be stuck with him. He flipped open his computer and got on Facebook: Stuff for Sale in Winona. He went into the living room, snapped a picture of his boots and board, and loaded them onto the page.

"So, what do people do for work around here?"

Tabitha served up mounds of spaghetti, and they sat down at the kitchen table. She twirled spaghetti on her fork and considered.

"Work-study at the University, I don't know. Kwik Trip, tend bar, work at the food co-op."

"I've got to figure out a gig where I can get quick cash."

"There's factory work around here, but I think you have to go through an agency."

"How bad does the snow get here?"

"Sometimes we get a lot." She pushed her plate to the side and half-closed her eyes. "I'm gonna crash early. I still feel like I'm jet-lagged from not sleeping on the bus."

"Yeah, me too." He wanted to lie down, put his feet up, but knew the next move. "I'll do the dishes. I really appreciate the pasta."

She hesitated.

"Really, I'll wash up and just leave stuff on the rack."

"Cool." And Tabitha smiled and headed upstairs.

He squirted soap into the sink and filled it with warm water. He'd never washed dishes at a restaurant before, but how hard could it be? Did places want an online application, even for that? He thought about Acoustic Café. Maybe he could try there tomorrow. He finished the dishes, folded the dishtowel on the counter, lay down on the couch to finish making his Facebook post, and fell asleep.

HE SPENT THE FOLLOWING DAYS asking about jobs at any place it seemed possible to get hired. Everyone was hiring "in a few weeks." The veterinary office downtown would consider having him walk dogs or clean out cages, but they wanted references, and he didn't know how to reach his manager from his lifeguard job.

The incoming storm made him feel trapped, but people seemed inspired by the idea of snow: he sold his boots and board off the Facebook ad. After making arrangements to meet the guy at Tabitha's, he went to the café.

Inside, the smell of warm bread and steamed milk washed over him. He studied the chalkboard menu, then ordered a hoagie and claimed a spot at a table. He googled Amtrak and punched in Winona and Nashville.

Bingo. From Winona, he could take a train to Chicago, arrive in the afternoon, and an 11 p.m. bus could take him to Nashville. $147 student rate. He figured in his head: he'd gotten $120 for the boots and board, and he'd just bought a huge sandwich; he still needed at least $40.

When he got up to put his basket back, he looked over the counter at the guy prepping sandwiches.

"Hey, do you know if they're hiring here—dishwashing, mop-up work? I'm broke and I need a gig."

The boy looked up. "I don't know, but you can ask." He pointed to a woman on the phone.

The woman had a ponytail and a headband like a college kid; she hung up, wrote something down, fielded Kevin's question about work, then plucked at a pair of brightly colored glasses hanging around her neck.

"Nothing here," she said, "but I've got three rental properties and the students are still away. We'll get snow tonight, so I'd pay you to shovel those sidewalks. Two of them are on corner lots, so you have to do both sides."

"I'm on it," he said. "Just tell me where to go."

"Do you have a car?"

He shook his head.

"They're not too far apart. Listen, I've got to finish some things here. Why don't you come in tomorrow morning, and I'll give you the addresses and point you in the right direction. There's shovel in the garage at each place."

"That'd be great. Hey, would you throw a few sandwiches into the deal?"

"Sure," she said. "No problem."

SNOW STARTED TO FALL as he walked back to Tabitha's. The town seemed peaceful; like a long exhale. Inside, Tabitha sat on the couch with a friend, the friend texting, her face hidden by a curtain of brown hair.

"What's up?" Tabitha asked.

"Got some food, got work shoveling snow tomorrow."

"Industrious."

"Gotta be."

"This is Vickie."

Vickie glanced up, "Hi."

"How'd you get work shoveling snow?"

"Boyish charm."

Tabitha smirked.

"A manager at Acoustic Café said she had some rental places."

"Nice."

"Yeah. Got sandwiches too. And I meant to ask before: how does a little town like this have a film festival?"

Vickie touched her phone and looked up. "The university hosts it—students can go for free. Last year, the best movie was about the gay rodeo. *Queens and Cowboys.*"

"What?"

She turned to Tabitha, "And Carl was in it—"

"What are you talking about?"

"Didn't you see it? Carl, my orientation teacher, had a part in it."

"No!"

"Yes! There's this whole gay rodeo circuit and someone made a movie about it."

"That's so cool!" Tabitha said.

WHEN KEVIN WOKE the next day, snow glimmered on the branches, on the mailboxes, everywhere. The world was serene. He needed coffee. He dressed and headed over to the café. Almost six inches of snow had fallen; people were shoveling already.

When he walked into the café, he ordered a tall cup of coffee and two muffins. A girl started to ring them up, and he looked for the manager, who nodded and told the girl she'd take care of it. She handed him a piece of paper with three addresses and a sketched map.

"Shoveling is serious business here." Kevin bit into a blueberry muffin.

"It's a legal thing. If someone slips outside your house because you haven't shoveled, you're paying his medical bills."

"Damn," he said. "I better get going."

NASHVILLE OCCASIONALLY got a storm that whitened things up, but he'd never shoveled snow like this before. He got a rhythm pretty quickly; the sidewalks were mostly even, and the snow was light where it hadn't been packed by walking. He thought about the film festival. It'd be fun to go, but he had to get back and see his mom; he didn't really want to visit her, but she'd be relieved to see him, and he owed her that, at least.

When he'd finished the last walk on his list, he looked around. A few houses still had snowy walks—maybe other people would pay for shoveling.

At the first house, no one was home. At the second, a hungover-looking student squinted at him, and Kevin could tell the guy had no money. At the next house, a little bunga-low, an old woman in a red cardigan came to the door. She didn't seem to understand his question.

"Never mind, hey, would you like me to shovel your walk? Just for free?"

"Oh, young man, that would be very nice." She crossed her arms and patted her own sweater sleeves; her knuckles were huge, her fingers angled almost like flippers.

He shoveled her path and the sidewalk in front of her house. She waved to him from the window.

He felt good. Better than he had in a long time.

At the next house, an angry-looking bald guy opened the door. "My snow blower is busted. And I just paid to have it fixed! I usually do Mrs. Donovan's walk for her."

"Does she live over there? I just took care of it."

"Did you charge her?"

"No, sir." Kevin couldn't think of the last time he'd said 'sir.'

"Good man. I'll pay you twenty-five bucks to do my walk and sidewalk and driveway."

Kevin looked at the driveway. It wasn't long, but it wasn't short either.

"Okay."

AS HE GOT TO WORK, the kids next door came tumbling out in snowsuits and boots and hats—they looked ready to tackle the Klondike.

"Hey mister, shovel it over here so we can make a fort!"

Mister. Wow. Kevin started pitching the driveway snow in their direction. They laughed and waved their arms. A little boy, waddling like a penguin, started wailing. "My mitten! Where's my mitten?"

His older brother laughed. "You don't need it."

"I need it for snowballs!"

Kevin felt a guilty start—had he covered it up with snow? He walked over to their yard.

"Dude, don't get worked up, I bet it's here." He used his shovel to pull away a clump of snow, and there was a blue mitten. Genius.

The kid held out his arms, Frankenstein-like. Both cuffs had clips to keep mittens attached, but one clip was open, filled with snow. Kevin had forgotten about those things. When he was little, he'd always lose his hats and gloves, which pissed his mother off. He had these mitten-clips, or whatever they were called, but at a certain point he refused to wear them. That winter, almost every day, his mother sent him off to school with a hat and gloves, and he'd come home without either. Kevin slapped the snowy mitten against his leg, cleared the snow out of the clip, and clamped it onto the mitten. He worked the mitten onto the kid's hand.

"There you go!"

The kid smiled shyly, then reached for a clump of snow, aiming at him and grinning.

BY THE END OF THE DAY, Kevin had shoveled a bunch of walks, returned the shovel to the house he'd taken it from, and collected two sandwiches from Acoustic Café along with his money. He went back to Tabitha's to thank her, and tell her he'd raised enough for a ticket home.

THE FOLLOWING MORNING, waiting at the railroad station, he wondered what it would be like to stay in a place completely by accident. If he hadn't had equipment to sell, he'd be stuck. Tabitha had saved his butt, but he was merely a funny story she'd tell on future ski trips.

Since he had to change in Chicago, he'd texted a friend from high school, Ezra, who lived there. It would be good to see him—even for a few hours between the train and the bus. Kevin hiked his pack onto his shoulder. He tried not to think about visiting his mom.

As the train left town, the tracks dipped low, close to the river. The Mississippi, wide and gray, glazed with ice, had backwaters broken up by sandbars and small, forested islands. On the far side, the bluffs stood stark and mountainous. Melissa would like this; she'd majored in geology and worked with water conservation or reclamation or something. He realized it was stupid that he didn't actually know what she did.

When they were kids, they used to goof around with a Canon Powershot he'd gotten for his birthday. He'd make little movies and edit them on his computer. Melissa was willing if not imaginative. He constructed scenes that didn't rely on her talking, and sometimes, he'd set up a visual joke she wasn't aware of until she saw the movie herself. He liked choosing music that didn't fit too neatly—that was one of his peeves: obvious sad music in the sad place, scary music to signal tension, it was dumb—music should work by juxtaposition rather than illustration. He liked to play with fades and transitions. Even his parents had liked those little movies. His dad would put his hand on Kevin's shoulder, lean over his laptop and say, "Play it again."

WHEN HE STEPPED onto the platform in Chicago, the smell of diesel smoke and fried food was like a shot of adrenaline. A text from Ezra:

```
Meet me at the Art Institute
Where?
So. Michigan Ave. 1 mile down Wabash
K
```

Chicago felt like a real city. Nashville, so imbued with its own sense of itself, felt provincial, like a large small town. The wanting and competitiveness among all the aspiring musicians and songwriters bled into the air, and of course Vanderbilt had its own traditions and history. He'd like to live somewhere without the past constantly in his face.

The Chicago Art Institute announced itself with banners and broad stone steps. Clumps of people stood in the somber afternoon, and Kevin scanned the sidewalk before recognizing Ezra, whose blond uncombed hair was longer now. With a scraggly beard, skinny jeans, and black Chuck Taylors, he was an urban version of his high school self. His arm draped over the shoulders of a girl with crimson hair; they studied something she held in her hand. Kevin called his name, and Ezra looked up.

"Hey, you made it," Ezra said. "Kevin, this is Rhonda."

Spiders crawled through her ruby-tinted hair. Kevin squinted. Bobby pins with little fake spiders on top.

"Nice spiders."

She grinned. "Let's go in. I'm freezing."

"Can we get coffee?" Kevin asked.

"Yeah, there's a place inside," Ezra said.

They started up the steps.

"So, did you really get on the wrong bus?"

"Yeah."

Ezra smiled out of the side of his mouth.

"I lucked out—this girl let me crash on her couch."

Inside, Ezra led them towards coffee. The museum was light and airy, filled with people, and Kevin felt cheered, as if he was somehow getting back on track.

"So, you're not going back to school this semester?" Ezra sipped his coffee and grimaced.

"Naah. I lost my ride. My mom's in rehab, so I don't get a tuition waiver."

"No shit. Your mom?"

"Yeah, that's what we've all been saying."

"Sorry, man."

"It sucks, for her I mean, and that's partly why I've got to get back. I think having a visitor—even me—might help."

"Some rehabs are nicer than others," Rhonda said. "Rehabs for doctors are posh."

"It's been kind of … startling. I'm supposed to be the fuck-up." He grinned, half-expecting to be contradicted, but Rhonda simply waited for him to continue. "But it gives me a break. I mean, it made sense to go to Vandy while it was free, but I want to get out of there."

"What are you studying?" Ezra asked.

"Nothing. I've got no idea. I'd love to go to film school— not to be a big director, just to know how to do some of that stuff—but my parents would flip out."

"Columbia College has a film program," Rhonda said.

"Here in Chicago?"

"Yeah, it's got all kinds of stuff. Book Arts, Writing, Film…" Rhonda slapped the table. "Half my friends go there. C'mon, I want to see the Frank photos."

"Seriously, again?" Ezra had become the personification of languid.

"What's the exhibit?" Kevin asked.

"Robert Frank's *The Americans*."

"Photographs. They're brilliant," Rhonda said. "He took them during the 50s—he was on a Guggenheim and police officers in the South thought he was a vagrant. Jack Kerouac wrote the introduction to the book."

Ezra smiled as if indulging a child. "They really are pretty good," he said.

THE BLACK AND WHITE photographs had a velvet darkness. Kevin lingered in front of one photo: "Trolley New Orleans—1954." The white faces in front, pruny and disapproving, the black faces in back, a buxom woman in her Sunday coat. A little white girl sat in front of a sorrowful-looking black man. A wavy chiaroscuro filled the top windows of the bus. Kevin thought how satisfying it would be to capture something like this, to frame what others didn't recognize and make them see it.

OUTSIDE THE MUSEUM, Ezra, smelling of cigarettes and patchouli, slung an arm around Kevin's neck. "Y'all come back now, you hear?"

"I just might." Kevin grinned.

ON THE BUS BACK to Nashville, Kevin dozed in the throb of oncoming headlights. Maybe he should move here, get a job, see what he could do. His dad was always asking, *What's your game plan?* as if somehow, overnight, Kevin would wake up and have one. Occasionally, his father would say that

Kevin could get a job in the warehouse at 3M, as if this was a job for a dolt who didn't go to school, but maybe he could actually do that for a couple months. If he worked full time between now and maybe April, he'd make bank. His mother would be out by then.

WHEN HE GOT OFF THE BUS, he spent his last few dollars on a Uber home. Inside, the house felt vacant. The refrigerator was empty. He texted Mel.

```
Home
You'll see Mom, right?
Yup
You have to let them know you're coming.
She put you on the list.
Glad I made the cut.
Good luck.
```

HIS DAD HAD LEFT HIM his mother's car keys and the address of the clinic. It felt strange and luxurious to get in a car with complicated temperature controls and leather seats. The clinic was on the other side of the city, a little outside of town, and the road curved past sparse forest and large homes. His hands twitched as he pulled into the parking lot. The building was modern brick and glass, like a hospital, but the plants out front, faux domestic touches, seemed like a bad disguise. He had to be buzzed in. A woman at the desk said his mother would be out.

Everything was pastel and chrome, windows and soft light.

When his mother came through the door, she looked smaller, diminished. No jewelry, no makeup. Her blonde hair was gray. It was strange to see her without the armor of perfection.

"Hi, Mom." He hugged her awkwardly, aware of his height. She smelled like a familiar soap or shampoo, and the normalcy comforted him. "You lead the way. Where can we talk?"

"The cafeteria."

He must have raised an eyebrow.

"Open space, so we can't have anyone bring drugs in."

He followed her, a half step behind, down a mauve hallway with bright artwork, into a room with round tables. A few other people were grouped at tables around the room. A pitcher of water and paper cups sat in the middle of a table, and she poured each of them a cup. He sat down next to her.

"I should have brought you a real cup of coffee."

"You wouldn't be allowed to bring anything in."

"Oh." It felt strange to be at a loss for words. So many times he'd wished she would just be quiet, but talking was all there was now. "This might sound weird, but what do you *do* all day?"

She twisted her mouth. "We have NA meetings, physical therapy, individual therapy. Group. Yoga. We have to exercise. Guest speakers. We stay pretty busy."

He started to ask if there was anything good about it, then realized what a stupid question that would be.

"You start to realize how much of your life was centered around your addiction. It's been…" she spread her hand out onto the table, then looked away. She shook her head.

The scent of fabric softener wafted by him. He tried to brush it away.

"I don't think your life was centered around that, it was around work and teaching, and us—"

Her smile was wan. "No, I'm afraid it was about hiding, about making everything look right, and trying to smooth the way for you and Melissa, which was folly, of course." Her face crumpled like a dead flower. "I haven't been a good mother."

"Mom, how I am is not your fault."

She sniffed. "Not completely. But I didn't help. It sounds silly, but I really didn't know how controlling….oh, it's embarrassing, this recovery jargon… how controlling I really was." Her lips wobbled, and she took a sip of water. "I thought I knew best about… well, everything." And then she started to cry.

He moved his chair closer and put his arm around her. Her shoulder blades felt bony under his arm.

"I shouldn't have given you medicine as a kid. I should have let you run around more." She gasped. "We should have sent you to a school that lets kids bounce on yoga balls … or lie on the floor, or…."

His pulse pounded in his head. He tried to take a deep breath. No one seemed to notice his mother's tears, but he wished she would stop.

"Mom, I hate to tell you this, but after a certain point, I didn't take anything. All that time you thought I taking stuff, I was flushing it."

She stopped crying for a moment, sat up and looked at him. Her gray eyes were teary, but assessing; recalibration, clouded by doubt, moved across her face.

"Really?"

"Yeah, really." He knew this wasn't the time to mention how much Adderall he'd sold or given away over the years.

She turned away and started to cry again, silently.

"It's okay." He took her hand. "It's okay." He knew it wasn't, but didn't know what else to say. When she had stopped crying, and wiped her eyes and blew her nose, he began again. "I don't know if you'll think this is funny or not—" and as he opened his mouth, he realized maybe he shouldn't tell her how wasted he'd been. "I got on the wrong bus in Colorado and ended up going to Minnesota instead of Nashville."

"Minnesota? How did you get home?"

"I ended up in this town called Winona, and I sold my boots and snowboard, and shoveled a bunch of walks to make money. I took the train to Chicago and a bus back to Nashville. So, who knew? You can get from Minnesota to Nashville for cheap."

He described his Russian seatmate's amusement at his predicament, and seeing Ezra in Chicago, and Rhonda's creepy but interesting bobby pins, and his mother laughed at his descriptions, blinking through her tears.

"So, Mom, I'm thinking about something—"

Her face made an inquiring mask, as if trying to stifle her first reaction.

"I'm thinking about moving to Chicago."

"What would you do there?"

"I don't know. Live for a while. Do a job and save up some money. Columbia College has a film program. You know, production stuff. You make movies as part of your coursework."

She put her hand on his arm. "Sweetheart, anything that makes you feel optimistic, that's what you should do."

"I'm going to ask Dad if I could get a gig in shipping or the warehouse for a few months. I'd save up some money, and I wouldn't leave while you were still in here."

"That's very sweet." She tried to smile. "They really want us to come out of here changed." She looked at him directly, then turned away. "I can't imagine going back right now, everyone knowing."

He'd assumed she'd do anything to get out; her embarrassment frightened him. "Well…people are going to know. They'll just have to get used to it."

"None of this is anything like what I thought it would be."

"I think that's how everything is," Kevin said.

WHEN THEY SAID GOODBYE, he hugged her for a long time and kissed the top of her head. He wondered if the gray had come on quickly, or if she'd just stopped dyeing it.

"Thank you so much for coming, sweetheart."

"Sorry it took me so long to get back here." It felt strange to stand there, not knowing how to say goodbye. He wanted her to feel better. "I know this is supposed to be some big self-examination time, but you know, we're all just doing the best we can."

Her lips trembled. A teary smile seemed the bravest expression she could muster.

OUT IN THE PARKING LOT, he started her car. January in Nashville was muddy and dank. He thought about Chicago's smoky buzz and Winona's crisp air. He liked shoveling snow, feeling the warmth inside his clothes while the air was cold. He thought of the old lady whose walk he'd shoveled, the way she'd watched him from her window, as if it didn't surprise her that random people might take care of her.

He stopped at the end of the driveway. To the left, the road bent sharply. Across the street, a convex mirror, mounted on a tree, let drivers see oncoming traffic. He remembered being small, his mother holding his mittened hand. She taught him to look both ways before crossing the street. Cautiously, he pulled forward, his eyes on the mirror, making sure that no one was coming, making sure the road was clear.

Acknowledgments

Thanks to the editors of the magazines who first published these stories. Special thanks to the editors at *River & Sound Review* for their insightful comments; Rick Peabody, for his abiding example; and Peter Stitt and Kim Dana Kuperman for publishing such a beautiful journal. My gratitude to Ann Patchett and the folks at *Crazyhorse*, now called *Swamp Pink*.

"Lovejoy" in *Carpe Articulum*; reprinted in *Best Fiction*

"Protect and Serve" in *Swamp Pink* (formerly *Crazyhorse*)

"Spillover" in *Gargoyle*

"Underwater Adventure" in *The Gettysburg Review*

"Look Both Ways" in *Lost Lake Folk Opera*

"Listeners at the Still Point" in *Mizzou*

"Flying in the Dark" in *Packinghouse Review*

"Collateral Damage," originally titled "John Kerry Kills Babies to Pay for the War in Iraq" in *River & Sound Review*

"And Not to Have is the Beginning of Desire" in *The Tahoma Literary Review*

Big thanks to SEMAC (Southeastern Minnesota Arts Council), which provided grants that afforded me the time to write "Underwater Adventure," "Flying in the Dark," and "Look Both Ways."

Thanks also to the Minnesota State Arts Board, which awarded funds through their Career Initiative Grant program.

The title "And Not to Have is the Beginning of Desire" is taken from Wallace Stevens' "Notes Toward a Supreme Fiction."

Finally, my gratitude to Dr. Ross Tangedal for his faith in this book, and Brett Hill for his sharp editorial eye.

Elizabeth Oness is a poet and fiction writer who lives on a biodynamic farm in Southeast Minnesota. Her stories have received an O. Henry Prize, a Nelson Algren Award, and the Crazyhorse Fiction Prize. Her books include *Articles of Faith* (2000), *Departures* (2004), *Twelve Rivers of the Body* (2007), *Fallibility* (2008), and *Leaving Milan* (2014). Oness directs marketing and development for Sutton Hoo Press, a literary fine press, and is a professor of English at Winona State University.